BUCHANAN TAKES OVER

Buchanan was a peace-loving man. But there was little peace in his life. Trouble just seemed to follow him. Like now. All Tom Buchanan wanted to do was pay a visit to young Nora and her family, and all hell broke loose. Between the crooked sheriff and the starving Indians bent on vengeance, Buchanan had his hands full. Everybody was out to get him, including a shady lady whose past was catching up with her.

JONAS WARD

BUCHANAN TAKES OVER

Complete and Unabridged

LINFORD
Leicester

First Linford Edition
published December 1989

Copyright © 1975 by Fawcett Publications, Inc.

British Library CIP Data

Ward, Jonas
    Buchanan takes over.—Large print ed.—
Linford western library
I. Title
813'.54[F]

ISBN 0-7089-6772-8

Published by
F. A. Thorpe (Publishing) Ltd.
Anstey, Leicestershire
Set by Rowland Phototypesetting Ltd.
Bury St. Edmunds, Suffolk
Printed and bound in Great Britain by
T. J. Press (Padstow) Ltd., Padstow, Cornwall

1

COMING up onto the high plain was always pleasurable, and Tom Buchanan drank the clean, cool air with gratitude. He had long been away from the nearby town of Encinal and his young friends, the Billy Buttons. There was a new baby, their first, and he was more than anxious to see them all.

The big horse, Nightshade, seemed also to enjoy the ride. His black hide shone in the sun. He nickered at the odor of piñon nuts fallen ripe from the little trees and pretended to shy at the shadow of a flying hawk. They came to a cool creek and Buchanan reined off the road and loosed the bridle so that the horse could drink.

Upstream a bit, Buchanan dipped his hands and rinsed them, then managed a few sips of the clear liquid. He hunkered down for a moment, wiping his brow.

He was sandy-haired, florid of

1

complexion. He was six feet four and ax-handle wide, scarred with the wounds of many battles he had not sought. Today was his idea of perfect, the weather fine, the sun warm but not too hot, the road stretching to an anticipated rendezvous with friends. He was a peaceable man.

He never wore a sidearm unless the occasion absolutely demanded it—he kept gun and belt wrapped in his saddlebag. His rifle was bonneted on the saddle where it might be needed anytime in this great Western countryside. He had thought to kill a deer and bring in the meat to his hosts, but there had been no opportunity.

There were gifts for the infant, of course, purchased in El Paso: a rattle, a rag doll, a cunningly carved, tiny wooden Colt 45. His money belt was well-filled with currency and his latest wound had completely healed. He was a happy man this early summer's day. As Buchanan slid Nightshade's bridle back in place, he looked westward to the Black Range, where he hoped to hunt and fish in the near future.

There was a smoke sign. He squinted, trying to read it, or to partially understand it since even Tom Buchanan could not always translate Apache signals. Back at Deming an oldtimer had said that Juju might be out, that it was the season for the fighting Apache, but no one had paid much attention.

Nightshade whinnied, a note of alarm. Buchanan dove for the horse, unwrapped the Remington, and mounted, all in one grizzlylike motion. There was movement in the gully beyond the running water. Buchanan kneed the big black and rode.

He charged directly toward the small canyon. He knew better than to run from Apaches when they were that close. An arrow in the back long years ago had taught him that lesson. He came in, rifle ready, holding fire, desiring to make absolutely certain that it was enemy Indians stalking him. A figure leaped up and fired a musket almost in his face. The noise

3

was tremendous but the bullet missed its mark.

Buchanan swung the rifle barrel, leaning down. Metal struck skullbone. Nightshade nimbly leaped a fallen log. Small brown-skinned men were running up the side of the depression, nimbly, as though they were on flat land. Buchanan dropped a shot among them, not aiming, not wishing to kill anyone who did not sorely need killing. They vanished, and he rode back to where his assailant lay flat on his face, arms outspread, blood seeping from his scalp.

When Buchanan was within arm's reach, kneeling to examine the extent of the damage he had inflicted, the prone figure moved. With the speed of a snake the Apache stabbed a long, sharp knife at Buchanan's vitals.

The big man did not move his feet. Only his bearlike paw reached for the sinewy brown wrist. He held the young man negligently, in a grasp so viselike that the stoic bravery slipped and the Indian winced, groaning.

4

Buchanan said, "Expected it. You of the People do not quit."

The youngster spat. "Pig-dog. White-eye. Skunk-stink."

"Juju has sure got you boys riled up. Wonder what it is this time?" He peered closely at the youth. "Hey! No wonder you got all that bile in you. White blood, shows plain." He stared again. "I'll be uncle to a buffalo. You're kin to Juju."

The boy braced himself, the blood still running down his café-au-lait cheek. "Juju is my father. You will die for this!"

"Uh-huh," Buchanan said. "Juju liked to kill me several times."

The boy spat. His English was slurred but quite plain. "You and your kind cannot be trusted. You are pigs!"

"Missions. They teach the language but they don't do much good." Buchanan now took the knife away from the numbed hand. "Like a razor, ain't it? You sure are one belligerent tyke."

He spun the youth around, noting that the body was emaciated, that the thin, strong arms were stringy as the calves of the legs. He dragged the boy to where Nightshade stood and found leather pigging thongs in his saddlebag. He tied the hands and feet and picked up the body as though it were a sack of wheat and carried it to the stream.

"Got to knock you people about to get a chance to take care of you," he said, ignoring the Spanish and American oaths issuing from the slit of mouth. "Trouble with yawl is you ain't got the brains of a duck, exceptin' to when it comes to trackin' or huntin' or fightin'."

He washed the wound, squinted at it. The young Apache was stone-faced now, enduring the pain in silence. Buchanan went back to his capacious bags and took out a clean linen cloth. He rummaged for a salve that a Crow Indian girl had given some time before and made a poultice. A trace of wonder showed, willy-nilly, on the face of the boy. Buchanan finished adjusting the bandage, untied the boy's hands and feet, and stood grinning at him.

6

The youth said grudgingly, "I am Jo-san."

"I am Buchanan. Tell your father that you met me," Buchanan advised him. "Tell your father to raid some place else or I might come after him."

"You would not dare!"

"Just ask your papa," Buchanan said. "Now, I'm visitin' friends hereabouts. You savvy Billy Button?"

"I savvy the white pig."

"You stay away from him and his baby and his wife," Buchanan said and now his words were strong and harsh. "You tell your papa what I say."

The boy came to his feet. He was older than Buchanan had first imagined, a full-fledged warrior, probably twenty or twenty-one. He wore Apache leggins, and now he plucked his red headband from the ground and stood as tall as he could manage, facing Buchanan. "You cannot buy me," he said. "Not with your bandages, with your words. You should have killed me. I will remember you, Buchanan."

"So will your old man." Buchanan was weary of the fanatical youth. "So will whole heaps of live Apaches. The dead ones, they don't remember. I am your friend. But when you come at me with your weapons I will kill you. And if you harm my friends I will kill you. That is enough!"

The boy swelled like a frog but could not find words. Of a sudden he leaped with the speed and agility of a mountain lion. In a trice he was astride of Nightshade, uttering the screaming, banshee howl that never failed to start horses running.

Nightshade quirked one ear, looked inquiringly at Buchanan. The youth called Jo-san kicked his heels. Nightshade reared, made a neat half-turn, then dropped his head and thrust his hind legs high, as though in play.

Jo-san flew through the air with the greatest of ease, reminding Buchanan of a trapeze artist from a circus he had once attended. At the end of a parabola the head of the Indian youth was thrust deep into a clump of purple furze alongside the stream.

"Enough of this nonsense," Buchanan said. "You go tell your papa I said so."

He climbed aboard Nightshade. The horse snorted, then resumed leisurely passage toward Encinal. Birds sang again in the trees. A giant butterfly paused curiously to look upon the rear end of the dazed Jo-san, then jittered upon its way.

Young Apache braves were sensitive, Buchanan knew. This one, being part Mexican, was extremely so, and it was a shame that he should have so far overreached himself. Still, there was nothing to be done about it. Jo-san could be as deadly as a grown brave—or a rattlesnake. His father was a strong, independent man, his mother a proud Mexican woman, once a slave, now the number one wife of the minor chieftain. There was a lot to be said for Juju and his like, and Buchanan had said it, over and over, to the authorities—but to no avail. Too many still believed the only good Indian was a dead Indian.

The road to Encinal grew wider than he remembered. It was a couple of years since he had passed this way and this was fast-growing country. The fields that had been forests were crisscrossed with canals fed by the waters of the mountain streams. Regular, straight rows of vegetables and grain and whatnot grew where none had grown before. Progress, they called it, taming of the land. People moving in, taking over nature and all its resources. Not for Buchanan, he thought sadly, not for his kind.

Now the birds and the bees and beasts were silent once more. He heard the sound of creaking leather and horses and men talking loud on the afternoon air. Buchanan, solid, a giant of a man on a big horse, drew Nightshade aside, under a tree, to allow these folks passage.

They came, a motley crew, riding in a heap, no order. In the van was a handsome man in gray, sharp-featured, wearing a soft felt hat rakish, a feather in its band. He was dark, wearing a close-cut Vandyke and neatly trimmed mustache. He saw Buchanan and reined in, hand on hip, a military gesture.

"Sir, my name is Beaumont," said the man. "There were shots fired."

"You might say that." Buchanan surveyed the posse and decided it was no better than any other; that is, it was composed of idlers and drunks from the saloon. He had a vast disrespect for town posses.

"Juju is out," Beaumont said. "You might be in consid'able danger, ridin' alone."

The Southern intonation was strong, as if he curled the ends of the mustache when he spoke.

"Ran into a son of his, name of Josan," Buchanan said. "No problem."

"He fired upon you?"

"Accidental-like," said Buchanan. "I know Juju."

"You escaped their attack upon you?"

"Wouldn't put it that way. They've gone back into the hills." He gestured. "Good thing, too. With yawl bunched up like that, someone mighta been hurt."

"Bunched up?" Beaumont raised thick brows. "We are readying a cavalry charge. Redskins do not fancy cavalry, my friend."

"Cavalry?" Buchanan grinned. "Now, do tell. Cavalry, eh? Looks a bit ragged to me."

A man rode from the rear of the disorganized crew. He was astride a fine bay horse, a sober man, squinting.

"Buchanan?"

"Well, if it ain't Mr. Avery," said Buchanan. "How is the assayin' business? How's the mine goin' these days?"

"Very well indeed," said Ed Avery, a solemn man. "Welcome home, Buchanan."

The man in gray said impatiently. "We waste time. Are we going after Juju or are we not?"

Mr. Avery said, "Well, I'll tell you, Mr. Beaumont. I didn't hanker for this rangdoodle in the first place. Reckon I'll just ride back with Mr. Buchanan, here."

"And let this redskin savage get away again? You'll be sorry, sir. I promise yawl

12

will be sorry if we do not chase down this criminal and hang him from the nearest tree."

Buchanan rode Nightshade out onto the road. The man named Beaumont had a ringing voice. The people of the posse seemed hypnotized by him—or afraid to flout him for some other reason. They all signified that they were with him, by gum, to the finish.

Beaumont flashed his dark gaze to Buchanan. "We shall meet again, sir. At your disposal."

He spurred his horse. He rode very well but his seat was military, as Buchanan had guessed. The others straggled after him. Avery sat on an old livery hack and shrugged.

"There he goes. Always raisin' hell about somethin'. He's kinda crazy, I think. The war, y' know? He was a Confederate soldier when he was just a lad."

"One of the new people in Encinal, eh?"

"Town has grown," said Avery. "Like

every other place. All the new farms. The mines are still producing."

"Nora doin' all right?"

"Just fine. You haven't seen their house, have you? Wouldn't know your way around, tell the truth. The store and the saloon—they've all been rebuilt. We got a bank. There's law and order and everything."

"Where's the marshal if he's not with the posse?"

"Beaumont," said Avery. "He's the marshal."

"Elected?"

"Yep. He talks a whole big lot," said Avery.

"And Billy?"

Avery hesitated. "Well, since the baby's born . . . Billy's in the new saloon a lot. Cards. I been worried—you know I handle the mine money and all."

Mr. Avery did, indeed, handle the money from the mine, which Mousetrap Mulligan had discovered up in the Black Range and in which Buchanan had a small share. Nora and Billy had run away to get married when they were both eighteen, and now they were twenty and parents and, if not wealthy, at least without financial worry. Every so often Mr. Avery sent a share of the take from the mine to Buchanan and once in a while a note. It was his latest laconic but informative letter that had been at least part of the reason Buchanan was returning to Encinal.

He said, "Thanks for lettin' me know about things, Ed. Has Coco Bean showed up yet?"

"I've been looking for him since you mentioned he was going to meet you here. He hasn't arrived."

"He had a fight in Tucson," Buchanan said. "He'll be along."

"I heard he knocked out a white man over there," said Avery.

"White, black, yellow, green . . . Coco knocks 'em all out," said Buchanan. "He's the black champion of the West. He'd be the white champion too, only they won't fight him for the title. Nobody's ever beat Coco."

15

"That's what I hear." Mr. Avery paused, coughed, then said, "Marshal Beaumont, he doesn't cater to the notion. He says niggers . . . black men . . . are animals. Like apes. He says they don't have room in their skulls for brains like other people. He talks like that a lot when people will listen. We don't have a single nigger left in Encinal."

"You had several in the mines if I remember."

"Yes. After Beaumont was elected they left."

Mr. Avery was certainly trying to convey something to him, Buchanan realized. He was making it clear enough, at that. Marshal Beaumont, late of the Southern army, was a man to be reckoned with. Also, he was a man who would certainly cross Buchanan at each and every moment of meeting. Also, Billy Button was not attending to his knitting, which would be his wife and baby and his mine and whatever other property he owned. Billy was still not quite twenty-one, and Mr. Avery acted for him when legally necessary. It was apparent that Mr. Avery was not entirely satisfied with matters as they were.

Buchanan said, "I'm mighty fond of those two. Nora and Billy. Mighty fond of 'em."

"I remember. Encinal was a tiny town in the hills. You had to fight Poley and Fanny. Desiderio and all them. Red Morgan died and you took care of Billy Button."

"It was a time," agreed Buchanan.

They rode on. Houses sprang into view, some neatly built, painted white. There was a knoll that had been unspoiled, empty except for the bushes and trees. Atop it now was a house larger than the others, with a high sloping shingle roof, a most expensive house for that part of the country. There was a garden and behind it a big barn. Avery reined in, pointed.

"Billy Button's place. Had everything sent in from the cities, furnishings too. Just them and a Mex gal and the baby, they rattle around some I reckon. Nothin' could stop him. He did want the best for Nora, her havin' the baby and all."

"It's a mighty fine house, seems like."

"Reckon you'll want to see it and them and the baby and all," said Avery. "I'll be in the office if you want to talk to me." He touched the brim of his hard round hat and rode away, a decent, honest man who had proved himself over the past couple of years.

There was a wagon road leading up to the house. Buchanan let Nightshade walk it. He looked around, observing a carriage house in addition to the neat red barn at the rear of the property, also a vegetable garden in the backyard. There was a shiny vehicle in the carriage house and a pair of matched bays in the barn. He dismounted in the stable yard and let Nightshade stand a moment.

Down below was Encinal. Where the saloon owned by the late one-legged Red Morgan had stood was a larger emporium bearing a big sign: PALACE HOTEL. Small adobe houses dotted the landscape, arranged in checkerboard fashion. The main street held stores and the bank. Avery's assay office was now surrounded with other enterprises where once it had been on the outskirts of town.

Behind Buchanan a voice cried. "Uncle Tom!"

He turned and Nora came running, throwing herself into his arms. She was no more than five feet tall and slight as a young birch. She looked no different from how he remembered her: bright-eyed, full of the joy of living, bouncing with energy.

He held her tight and said, "Been tryin' to get up here for a long while, now. Bless your little heart."

"Oh, Uncle Tom, I've missed you so. How many times I've wanted to talk to you, to be with you, to know your whereabouts."

"Come on, now, it ain't that bad." He laughed and pushed her off to arm's length. He saw a slight trace of sadness, a mere shadow in her eyes. He said, "Whatever it is, you just let it come out whenever. Meantime, didn't I hear tell somewhat about a young un?"

19

"Come on," she cried and the shadow vanished. "Hurry. He's probably eating us out of house and home right this very minute."

They went in the back way. Nora had been wearing a sunbonnet in the garden, which did not match her overalls; now she doffed it and her hair hung in braids as before. She was twenty and looked no more than sixteen, he thought.

The kitchen was huge. A Mexican girl sat at a long table. In her arms was a tiny bundle that made demanding noises. The girl had a spoon in her hand and was poking some kind of mush into the yammering mouth.

Nora said, "He always wants me to feed him. We're trying to break him. He's like a hard-mouthed bronc."

Buchanan removed his sombrero. He walked around the table on tiptoes. He was somewhat scared, he found. Babies were way out of his line.

He had been on the frontier all his life. His lawman father had been slain, his mother had died. He had never been close to marriage himself. Nora and Billy had been about all the family he could claim since he was a teenager. This addition was a novelty.

Nora was saying, "Teresa, this is Uncle Tom Buchanan. You've heard us speak of him often enough."

She was a pretty girl with coiled black hair and limpid brown eyes. "*Sí señor! Sí*, Oncle Tom. Thees is Billy Hoonior." She held out the baby.

Buchanan recoiled, putting his hands behind him. He stared at the plump red face of the infant, the beady eyes plainly resenting this interference with the process of feeding.

Nora said. "His name is Thomas Mulligan Button."

"Sonofagun." He suddenly found himself holding the baby on the palm of his left hand, balancing it with the right. "Looks like his old man!"

"He's beautiful. Ain't he beautiful?" Nora gazed upon the little bundle with adoring eyes.

"Beautiful?" Something told Buchanan

to lie. He was a man of peace and it was often diplomatic to evade a harsh truth. "Why, sure. He's as beautiful as . . . as . . . a piglet in a barnyard."

Teresa giggled. Nora looked taken aback for a moment, then she smiled.

"Nothing's cuter than a piglet," she said.

Thomas Mulligan Button wriggled. He reached out a hand and grabbed Buchanan's thumb. He hung onto it, grunting and squirming. His toothless mouth curled in a wide grin, his beady eyes stared straight at Buchanan. He began to talk. It made no sense at all, but his intentions were of the best.

Nora crowed, "See? He knows you already. He's tellin' you something."

"I think he also is a little bit like his grandpa, Mousetrap," Buchanan said. "You mind how he talked a heap, especially in his cups?"

"That's how come his name. Thomas Mulligan. For you and for Grandpa," said Nora. "And you're in time for the christenin'. Fact is, we been postponin' it, hopin' that you'd show up at last."

"Christenin'?" This was new to Buchanan.

"In the church. We got a church now. Miz Avery, you remember her, she's the preacher."

"I be doggone." He stared helplessly at Thomas Mulligan Button. The baby pursed his lips, emitted a large bubble and a sound patently disrespectful. The Mexican girl giggled again, and Buchanan thrust the infant at her. Young Button went willingly, possibly eagerly. "Uh-huh. Some baby."

Nora was dancing, not yet finished with her wonders to display. "Come on, now. Upstairs. Follow me!"

He climbed a wide stairway. The house had been built well, he saw. There was a hall and rooms on each side of it and evidently a room down at the end. She pranced down to this door and opened it. Buchanan stared.

"A bathtub and all? Glory me, you really did get fancy, you kids."

"Water pumped up from our spring," she said. She pulled a chain and a cascade erupted into a chamber. "Just like the big cities. We saw the first one in El Paso when we got married, and Billy said he had to have one if it took a fortune. It near did."

"But the claim does pay off." There had been some doubt after Buchanan had blown up several people and the possible source of Mousetrap Mulligan's Golconda in defense of their lives.

"Yes. You just got to take a bigger share, Uncle Tom. You just got to."

"No," he told her, grinning. "I don't got to do any such of a thing. You wanta make me lazier 'n I am?"

But she was off again, her tiny feet twinkling down the hall. She threw open another door. "Come see your room! Your very own!"

He went and paused on the threshold. It was a big room. In it was a bed, covered with a hand-quilted comforter. There was a big bureau. There were three chairs, two of ordinary dimensions, one oversized and wide-armed and comfortably designed for Buchanan. There were Indian rugs on the floor and Mexican blankets adorning the walls. On one wall was a huge canvas painted by an artist who was not entirely comfortable in his medium.

The painting was of Mousetrap Mulligan's claim at the time of the fight with Poley and Fanny and the renegades. It was supposed to show Nora and Billy and Buchanan as they defended themselves against great odds. The explosion of the dynamite, which saved the day, seemed a part of the background, but truly if it had been that close, none of the three would have survived. It was a case of getting too much detail into one frame.

Still, it was recognizable. It told the end of the story, after Nora had been rescued from captivity, after Billy had proven himself more than a tough, bigmouth kid, after the two youngsters had discovered they were in love. And Buchanan was twice as big as life, bleeding from a leg wound, handling his rifle.

He said, "Well, this is . . . this is . . . why it's home. First home I've had since I left East Texas."

"That's what we thought. That's why we been tryin' to get you here. Do you like it, Uncle Tom? Do you really like it?"

He hugged her under one big arm. "Why, a man'd be a pure dumb fool not to like it."

She said, "I only wish Billy was here to see you, to know you like it."

"Where is the little man?"

She laughed, shrugged. "Down at the saloon, I expect. Or out looking at the cattle. He never gets tired of looking at that prime herd he bought."

"Cattle?"

"On the plain, you know, the grama grass, where we had the big fight? Billy bought it. He's got Herefords and he's got a prime bull out there, whooee!"

"Well, that's fine."

She said, "You come on down and eat.

Then if Billy don't come home, you can go look for him. Okay?"

"I could eat." He looked around the room. "I'll just put up Nightshade and bring my gear . . . up to my room."

She put her arms around him as far as they would go, which was about halfway. She wept with joy. "That's what I wanted to hear you say. I wanted it so bad! 'My room.' That's what I wanted."

2

THE stage from Warm Springs pulled in with a flourish and stopped in front of the Palace Hotel. Coco Bean squeezed his bulk out the door and waited until the driver dropped a valise into his big, strong hands. The black champion of the western world surveyed the main street of the town of Encinal.

Coco wore a suit of brown and white checks, a sweater with a collar that rolled around his short, thick neck, a hard hat, and yellow shoes with knobby toes. On his left hand he wore a ring of gold encrusted with several large diamonds. He was not a figure to pass unnoticed.

He saw a town that fairly squeaked with newness, a town that was raw underneath but the surface of which was like an ice cream pie. All the buildings had been painted. Glass shone: the windows

28

of the bank, the general store, a jewelry shop. At the far end of the street a small church steeple reared against a proud sky. This was not the Encinal of which Buchanan had told bloody tales of death and desolation.

The stage driver, a friendly man named Jackson, said, "Hey, champ. I wouldn't ask for Buchanan in the hotel."

Coco looked at him for a moment, nodded understanding. "Reckon I know what you mean."

"Man name of Beaumont. Got a sister, real purty gal. He's the marshal. Was in the rebel army."

Coco said. "Do tell."

"Well, you·wouldn't want to get into that. Y' see there used to be plenty nigras in the mines. They all left when Beaumont got to be marshal."

Coco said, "A man I don't wanta meet. Just like you say, friend."

"You come here to fight McMillan?"

"Who he?"

Jackson shook his head. "If you don't

know it ain't true. Thought you might be fixin' to."

"I don't know him."

"Rassler-fighter. Big man. Bigger 'n Tom Buchanan."

Coco grinned, showing a gold tooth. "Now, you know better 'n that, Mr. Jackson. He might be *taller* than Tom Buchanan. He might be *wider* than Tom Buchanan. He might be *heavier* than Tom Buchanan. But there ain't nobody in this here ole world *bigger* than Tom Buchanan."

He picked up his satchel and went into the Bank of Encinal. He stood at the counter, watched several clerks at work. There was a door lettered HAMILTON MIZER, PRESIDENT. The hired help ignored Coco.

After a moment the door of the president's office opened and a lanky man wearing steel-rimmed spectacles emerged. He was very tall and very thin and his face was pinched like a prune behind the eyeglasses. He stared at Coco.

"Yes, boy? You have a message for me?"

Coco tipped his hard hat to one side. He reached into his coat pocket and took out a thick sheaf of paper money. "You don't mind, Mr. Mizer, I'd like to have you take care of this for me? Until I can get to talk with Mr. Buchanan?"

The clerks all stared. Mr. Mizer came and looked at the money. Adjusting his glasses, he held it up to the light, shuffling it bill by bill. It was crisp new money. Suspicion rode him like a hagmare.

"Where did you come by this money, boy?"

"Name of Coco Bean," he said softly. "I win it. Earn it. I whupped a white boy callin' himself Jesse James Junior. T'ain't his name, he just tryin' to make hisself real big. He just an ord'nary fighter. Can't take a good punch."

"I don't know anything about pugilism. It is illegal, as a matter of fact. Here, take your money."

Coco accepted the bills without

changing expression. He stacked them away and asked, "Could you tell me where to find Mr. Buchanan?"

"I don't know any Buchanan." Mizer was already on his way toward a safe at the side wall of the bank, a vault of impressive dimensions. "Good day, boy."

Coco looked around at all the people in the bank. He showed them his gold tooth again. He said, "Good day, ladies and gentlemen. It sure ain't been nice to meet yawl."

He went out into the sunshine. He walked next door to the Palace Hotel. His face was clear of anger; he had lived too long as a black man to show his resentment. He stood in front of the hotel, ruminating. It was a crazy world in a lot of ways. He was a champion at his trade. He was a friend of Tom Buchanan, one of the most respected—and in some quarters feared—men of the western frontier. He was a simple man of simple pleasures, never concerning himself with the affairs of others. Yet because his skin was black and in spite of the Emancipation Proclamation he was unwelcome on most levels of society to which he was exposed.

A company of horsemen came into town from the south. Their leader, a man in gray clothing, rode in a manner that told Coco he was unhappy and resentful. The others straggled, dropping off here and there from the caravan until only the gray man and one other were left. They tied up at the rack in front of the hotel. The gray man had a black mustache and short beard. The other man had a mean mouth and wore his guns low on each flank. Both paused on the walk and stared at Coco.

"Yes, boy? You want somethin' hereabouts?" asked the man in gray.

Coco sighed. "Just lookin' for Mr. Buchanan."

"Buchanan? Ah, yes. Buchanan." Now the two men exchanged thoughtful glances. "And a young man named Button?"

"That's right, Billy Button, friend of Mr. Buchanan."

"Yes. Well, just wait here a minute.

Don't go into the hotel, now. Just wait right here. Come on, Dolan." The gray man led the other man into the hotel.

Coco had glimpsed the star under the gray coat. The man named Dolan must be a deputy, he figured. The law. Jackson had warned him. Marshal Beaumont and Deputy Dolan. The secesh, they were, the kind who had enslaved Coco's ancestors. He opened and closed his hands, the valise between his yellow shoes. One more time today, once more they had called him "boy" and looked at him as though he were dirt . . .

A small young man came out of the hotel. He wore range clothing but not the kind you bought in the store; they were the kind they tailored for ranch owners. He wore a flat-topped hat with a rakish brim. His boots had especially high heels that made him look a bit taller but caused him to teeter on his toes. He had small, round eyes and he wore a beaming grin.

"Hey, you gotta be Coco Bean! I'm Billy. You know, Uncle Tom's Billy

Button." His hand was strong, lost in the mighty fist of the fighter.

The sun shone a little brighter, people passing in the street smiled and waved at Billy, a man called out that the posse hadn't caught sight of Juju or any other Indian. Billy grinned at them all.

Coco said, "Sure glad to meetcha. I was beginnin' to think this here wasn't no place for me to meet Tom Buchanan. Nor nobody else."

"You mean Elton Beaumont? Him and the deputy, Rack Dolan? Pay 'em no heed. You're my friend if you're friend to Uncle Tom. And nobody in Encinal gives me no trouble. C'mon, I'll buy you a drink while we wait for Uncle Tom."

Coco said, "The man said no."

"He did, eh? Sounds like him." Billy's round eyes became slits. "You and me, we're havin' a drink in the bar of the hotel. Right now."

"Me, I don't drink nothin' but milk nohow," Coco protested. "Druther not, please."

"Okay, you can have milk while I drink!"

Coco tried to explain. "Men wearin' guns. They don't like black folks. I don't like them and fact is, I'm plumb scared of guns."

"Don't be scared when you're with me. This here is my town," Billy said, sticking out his small chest.

Coco shook his head. "I done found a banker. Name of Mizer. He acts like he owns the world. That marshal and his deputy, you reckon they don't own part of the town? Now, I don't care whose town it is—I come here to meet Tom Buchanan."

Billy's mouth was a thin line. "I don't care what anybody says. I was here before all of them people. And if I say you drink in the Palace bar—it goes!"

Coco sighed. He knew all about white men who thought they were boss. He always allowed them their belief. Like his friend, Buchanan, he was basically peaceable. He truly feared guns and gun play. He stayed alive and happy by going along with the white people up to a certain point. But Buchanan many a time had to forcibly alter people's attitudes.

A lady came sweeping onto the veranda of the hotel. She was a small, dark woman with her hair parted in the middle and drawn back in coiled braids. Coco recognized a hairdo from the old South. She also had the ivory skin and wide eyes and air of brightness of the Southern lady. She was very pretty. Her chin was rounded and firm and you knew she was accustomed to having her own way, especially with men.

"Billy Button!" Her voice was soft, a bit arch, caressing. "What in the world you doin' standin' there with a friend? Come sit on the po'ch with me."

Billy beamed. "Miss Heloise, this here is Coco Bean, champion prizefighter. He's the one I told you about, my Uncle Tom's friend."

The lady's smile was warm, her teeth white and even. "Well, now, you two come right here."

Coco went reluctantly, with the realization that Billy would leave him standing alone if he did not follow. There were chairs on the long veranda, and they sat on either side of the lady.

She said, "I've heard of you, Coco. Indeed, I have."

"Thank you, ma'am." He was not happy but he maintained a sober, respectful mien.

Billy was saying, "Have them bring me a drink, Miss Heloise. And milk for my friend."

She clapped her hands, a pistol-shot sound coming from such a dainty lady. A man came onto the porch, slick-haired, slim, wearing a white shirt and tight-fitting striped pants. She said, "Daggett, have someone bring us drinks and a large glass of milk for Coco, here."

The man stared, then said, "If you say so, Missy."

Billy laughed, not pleasantly. "She said so, Daggett. She does own the place, don't she?"

Daggett had cold blue eyes. He turned

them briefly upon Billy, lifted one shoulder. A corner of his mouth curled. He went inside. Coco felt more and more uncomfortable.

"Milk," the lady was saying. "You *are* big and strong. Are you training for a bout of fisticuffs?"

"No'm. Just here to meet Mr. Buchanan."

"But you could meet Mac. Our Mac," she cried, clapping hands again. It seemed a favorite gesture. "Surely you've heard of Big Jim McMillan."

Coco said, "No'm, not until just today."

"But it would be advertising for Encinal!" she said. Her enthusiasm was contagious. Billy Button perked up, nodding as she went on. "The town is growing but not fast enough. The hotel—Billy knows. Without the bar . . . Well, enough. We must have a prizefight."

Billy explained to Coco. "Miss Heloise owns the hotel, y' see. And it's kind of ahead of its time. We don't get that many visitors yet. If it wasn't for the bar and the poker game she'd have a tough time."

"Now, Billy." She put a white hand upon his arm. "You been so good to us! I swear, without you we'd be lost."

Billy said, "Her brother, y' see, the marshal, well, he don't draw a big salary. Any time we can help the hotel, we're helpin' the town. Y' understand?"

"Oh, yes, indeed." He understood the hand that remained on Billy's sleeve, petting him. He understood the way Billy looked at the Southern lady. Buchanan had told him that Nora and Billy were the happiest of adoring couples, who had run away to be married in their teens, who had found their love in the crucible of mortal danger.

The man named Daggett came out, himself bearing a salver upon which were a straight whiskey, a glass of sherry, and a beaker of milk. He too had a military bearing. He had the air of one who had seen better times. But he did not seem to be a happy man. Coco accepted his beverage, watching, listening, slightly perturbed. Men came and went, all staring at him, at Miss Beaumont and Billy, coming into the hotel or departing. There were miners and ranchers and local businessmen. All spoke or waved to the lady and Billy. A giant of a man came down the walk.

He was bigger than Buchanan, at that. He seemed a size larger than anyone Coco had ever seen. His arms hung down to his knees. His face was wide and square and his eyes slate colored. He moved loosely and easily with none of the awkwardness of the average big man.

Heloise Beaumont cried, "There you are, Mac. Come here this minute. Come and meet Coco, the nigger champion!"

McMillan stood on the walk. He had a wide mouth. which twisted into a grin. "Coco Bean? You come here to fight me, didja?"

"Nope," said Coco. He did not rise, did not offer to shake hands. He was wary of this man in miner's clothing and hobnailed boots. "Come to visit."

Marshal Beaumont came onto the

41

veranda. He had changed clothing; everything he now wore was another shade of gray, even his neat walking boots. His star shone on a vest of moiré silk—gray in color. He nodded to McMillan, then turned a frown upon Coco seated beside Heloise. Coco did not stir.

Heloise said, "Brother, you've met Coco. Now, can't we arrange a fight with him and Mac? Is there no way we can promote this fine attraction?"

"Truly, my dear, not my business," said the marshal.

"Really?" Her voice became silken. Again she clasped Billy Button's arm. "Maybe we can manage without you, then. Maybe we can do something for the town without your sterling aid."

Beaumont pointed a finger. "You got a nigger sittin' next you on our veranda, darlin' sister. You havin' our people wait on him. You know how I feel about that."

"I don't care how you feel about it," she told him, still smiling, still demure. "It's my property, isn't it?"

He was expressionless. "The nigger

had better make himself scarce around here. I've suffered enough from the freein' of his people. I know enough about 'em."

Billy Button came up from his chair. "You know what, Elton? Mr. Marshal Beaumont? Whatever you want to be called. You don't own this town. You don't own nothin' in it. You're lucky you got a job and your sister gives you free room and board. What you want or don't want cuts no ice with me nor anyone else that amounts to anything in this burg. You understand that?"

Beaumont turned white. His voice was harsh with rage. "You are asking for trouble, young Button. Real trouble."

"I ain't carryin' a gun," Billy snarled. "Any time I am—you take your best shot. That badge don't mean a thing to me. You're just another hunk of trash from the South—beggin' your pardon, Miss Heloise. Comin' here talkin' about my friend Coco Bean, who could tear out your tongue for you with one hand. You're disgustin', Elton."

McMillan moved. "Hey, Billy. Happens Elton's a friend of mine."

Billy hooted. "Sure! You and Rack Dolan and Freddy Daggett and a few saddle bums and tinhorns. Those are his friends. He's a two-bit phony and if it wasn't for his sister he'd be run outa town before now. S'cuse me again, Heloise, but you know it's the truth. Marshal! He couldn't catch a cold in January much less Juju or the rustlers we know are in the hills."

Coco was watching the marshal. He expected a gun to be drawn at any moment. His stomach ached at the thought of guns. He would have departed forthwith excepting that he had no place to go. He did not know whether Buchanan had arrived. He looked at the lady, his instinct telling him that she could control the situation anytime she wished.

Beaumont drew a deep breath. "You're only a boy, Button. You don't know the meaning of danger. There will come a time."

He turned on his heel and walked down the street. McMillan loomed at his side.

They did not speak, walking together. There was a cantina at the end of the block. They turned into it. Coco looked at his two companions.

Heloise said, "You should not be so hard upon him, Billy. He is my brother, but I cannot always control him."

"He should mind his manners," Billy said. "I don't know why you put up with him."

"He's not evil. He's been hurt," she said. "The war—the things that happened after the war. And he's not a bad marshal. You shouldn't say he is."

"He made me mad."

She smiled serenely. "You mustn't get mad so easy. Isn't that so, Coco?"

"Best not to." But there was something wrong. The lady, her brother, the big fighter who moved like a cat, they were all off-key. Coco understood straight-forward people. Buchanan would have to figure out these people.

"Would you consider fighting Mac?" the lady was asking. "Please?"

"Well y' see I just had a bout. And . . .

Tom Buchanan, he arranges my affairs."

"Ah," she said. "I look forward to meeting Mr. Buchanan, truly I do."

"You will, Heloise, you will," Billy said. He touched her hand. "Best we go home now. Tom may be comin' in any time."

"See you later?" She had dimples when she smiled.

"You bet!"

She waved them away. She was a lady who gestured a lot, Coco thought, carrying the valise, walking down Main Street beside little Billy. She was a lady that needed watching. What she said had meaning. And her brother had killer eyes when he stared at Billy. It was all peculiar. Coco did not like it. He listened to Billy describing the town, the people they passed on the street, the prospects for a bigger and better Encinal, but his mind was on the Beaumonts and Daggett, and on McMillan, the giant who really was outsized, really was of greater proportions than Buchanan.

They came out the back door of the

46

cantina, the marshal and the giant. They walked the back lots to the hotel, speaking briefly in short sentences.

"You think he's easy?" asked Beaumont.

"Too little. I'll stab him to death," said the miner-prizefighter.

"Problem is to set it up with yawl."

"Not my problem."

"Heloise can do it."

"Mebbe."

"She's got that shrimp Billy right where she wants him."

"Got ain't keepin'. I seen hooked fish get away."

"She digs deep," said Beaumont. They went into a room at the back of the hotel, part storage and part office, a room kept locked from visitors or minor employees. There was a desk and a lamp and several barrel chairs were about. Heloise sat behind the desk. Freddy Daggett occupied a chair near her.

Heloise said, "You almost over did it, Elton. Hating Billy is one thing. Showing too much of it is another."

"The cocky little bastard should drop dead," said Beaumont viciously.

"Not until we get more of his money," she reminded them. "The little we milk from him in the poker games won't keep this hotel going. The gamblers in this burg won't help—there just are no real high flyers. If we are going to build up this property and unload it on some sucker, we need Billy. No matter which way we go—he's our ace in the hole. And you've got to apologize to him before the poker game or we'll lose him."

"Apologize hell!"

She clapped her hands. "You'll do it, you know. The minute he walks in here, you'll do it!"

Beaumont started to speak, stopped. Daggett lifted a shoulder, nodding at Heloise.

"You're right, as usual. And the prize-fight would help."

"I admit that," Beaumont said sullenly. "It would bring in people. We need people to spend money."

"I haven't picked a pocket in a year," said Daggett. "I'll have to practice."

"You'll have to be careful," Heloise said. "If we could score big, like maybe the bank or something, we could shake the dust of the damn town forever. Mizer's mortgage—there's no way we can meet it with things the way they are."

"Mizer's bank. That's a switch," said Daggett. "I like that. Mac knows about explosives."

Heloise said, "But the right time would be while he's in the ring . . . Can you see it?"

"I see it," said Beaumont. "Freddy learns quick. Maybe Mac could teach Freddy how to blow a safe."

"Then we could forget the hotel. It sounds good to say we're building the town, all that," said Heloise. "I think we've got something."

McMillan spoke for the first time. "Hey. I'm in the ring, fightin' the nigger. You hit the bank, grab the loot, duck the country. Where does that leave me?"

"You collect the purse, right?" Heloise

smiled at him. "You're in the clear. You join us in Canada and we divvy up."

Beaumont drawled, "Darlin', your Southern accent is slippin'. I declare, you'll hurt the ears of Freddy and me with that Yankee palaver."

McMillan said, "Nemmine that. I hear you, Heloise. It's a deal. I'll get some dynamite from the mine and show Freddy. He always picks things up quick and smart."

"We've done well," said Heloise. "I admit I made a mistake in the hotel. I thought we could work the field. These Westerners are too smart. What we can do isn't enough." She stared at Beaumont. "Elton, dear, we're here to make a killing, like always. But not to kill people."

He flushed. "Yankees. Niggers—"

She interrupted. "You hear me. I'd like for you to make the big score, buy back your old plantation, all that. I'm for it. But until then try and make it easier for the rest of us. We've been together a while now. Let's stay together."

He relented. "You're right as rain, darlin'. I'll do like you say."

"And I'll whup the black man," said McMillan. "And Freddy, he always comes through."

"Thanks," said Daggett. "Nobody knows about Mac bein' the best in the country—until he got caught in that bank with the safe door open. It ought to work."

"It always has," said Heloise.

It was time to break up the meeting; the men said goodbye. She had done it again, as she had so many times; she had poured oil on troubled waters. All would be well now until the next go-around.

She sighed. She was Heloise Dare, thirty years of age, she ruminated, and one day soon she would look it. It was a hideous thought. She had controlled men with her good looks, her enthusiasm, and her brains for a long time, now.

Her parents had died young, and she had found her way from Philadelphia to New York. She had dabbled in theatrics with little success. She had learned that older men had money and were susceptible to young beauties. She had learned the con game and was very good at it.

She had picked up Beaumont when he was on his uppers after the war, reduced to cheating at cards in small poker games. Beaumont had known Freddy Daggett, whose family had been famous and rich before the war, far more important than Beaumont's people. Both men were drifters, both had nerve, and both could provide a classy front.

McMillan had joined up after breaking jail in New Jersey. His real name was lost in time. He was indeed a very fine boxer —and a good safe cracker. He was their strong-arm man.

She had kept them together. She was the catalyst. She had once intended to marry Elton, but she had detected a flaw in his character before it was too late. Elton was a hater. It could bring trouble and in the end it was a self-defeating trait. Heloise could connive without hating.

Billy Button was another matter. She had him on a string. He loved his wife but he also craved excitement. He could not stay away from the poker table. And he had absolutely no experience in the world that would enable him to cope with a Heloise Dare-Beaumont. She could feel him tremble at her touch, see him grin at the wheedling of her phony Southern accent. She could tool him along for a while yet, at least until she did not need him.

She sighed. There was a bottle of whiskey in a drawer. She took it out and sipped from the neck of it, laughing a little—she never drank whiskey in public. She had her weaknesses. She faced them, admitted them to herself.

Her present ambition was to get back East and open a gambling hall in New York, protected by certain politicians of whom she knew more than they liked her to know. She had meant to milk the West, the innocent frontier people, for the capital she needed.

She was wary. The poker game was doing all right but not as well as she had hoped. She had not foreseen that the

Westerners knew the game better than most people. And then there was Mr. Mizer, the tight-wad banker . . .

The next problem, of course, was Billy's uncle Tom. Not that she worried about any male—she looked forward to meeting this man named Buchanan.

She had never seen the man she could not enchant. There were a dozen ways and she had learned them all in the various establishments where she had been employed during her formative years along the eastern seaboard. She had accumulated her Southern accent and a great deal of confidence in herself during these times. She had no fear of any male animal.

They sat on the cool porch in the evening, awaiting the call to dinner by Teresa. Buchanan's toys lay forgotten as Thomas Mulligan Button cooed and grinned toothlessly at Coco Bean. It had been love at first sight between them, the tiny pink baby and the big, husky black man.

Buchanan winked at Nora and said,

"I'm plumb jealous. When we have the christenin' I suggest you change his name to Coco Mulligan."

"He's jest a beauty, that's all," Coco said, cradling the infant. "Trouble is, you don't know nothin' about babies, you big cowboy fella."

The baby let out a delighted yip and bit Coco's index finger. The two laughed together and were happy, hugging each other. Billy rocked in his chair, bursting with pride.

Nora said, "He's a pure pleasure. Grows some every day, seems like."

"He'll be bigger 'n me by the time he's five," Billy said.

"Just so he's good and sweet," Nora said, gazing upon her offspring.

Billy said, "You didn't give me an answer about Coco and Big Jim McMillan. Could it be arranged?"

Buchanan looked at the black man, who shook his head. "I don't think so. Coco didn't take kindly to Encinal."

"You mean about old Mizer? And Beaumont, that four-flusher? Shoot,

Uncle Tom, that little old gal Heloise runs the hotel and Mizer, he's just the president of the bank. We could put our money in an El Paso bank by stage if we wanted to. Me and Miss Beaumont, we could put on the prizefight and draw a crowd from all over the territory."

"You don't know anything about prizefightin'," said Buchanan mildly. "Not about Coco, exceptin' what I have told you."

"He can beat Mac. I'll bet my last dime on it."

There was a small silence. Then Nora said a bit wearily, "He would, too. Our last dime."

"Now, Nora, don't you start that," said Billy. "Just because I lost a little in the last poker game."

"I just can't figure two thousand dollars as a little," Nora said. "I just can't get that into my head. I mind when Grandpa and me ate sourdough biscuits and beans for weeks at a time. I remember havin' one dress and no shoes at all. I couldn't ever forget."

"I don't want to remember them times," Billy cried. "We got what everybody wants. We got the claim and now I'm startin' a prime herd and we got this house and a mighty fine baby and all and people's jealous. That's the trouble. Jealous. The only friend I got in town is Miss Heloise because they're all jealous."

"I know . . . I know. You keep sayin' that," Nora said, turning away, reaching out to take the baby from Coco, holding it close.

Buchanan was silent through an awkward moment. He could remember when Billy had been a problem in the town, to Red Morgan—and to Buchanan. Someone had left the infant Billy on Morgan's doorstep, which had been the entry to a tough frontier saloon. Encinal had been a one-horse village where the miners and cowmen had come to Morgan's place for their booze and women, and this had been Billy's upbringing.

"Have to check around town later,"

Buchanan finally said mildly. "You got yourself some cattle, you say?"

"I got 'em and I got a bull that won't stop. You remember Mando?"

"The Mexican fella who helped us when we were havin' the trouble?"

"He's my foreman. I got *vaqueros* out there can handle anything that comes up, anytime. Includin' Juju and his Apaches or rustlers or anybody else."

"You hired Mexican help?"

"All the way. Mando brought 'em in. Fine boys. Nobody around here can touch 'em when it comes to cowboyin'."

"And how would you know?" Buchanan asked gently.

"I don't remember you havin' experience with cattle."

"I hired people to teach me. Mando's uncle and them. They been cowboyin' for hundreds of years."

"True, makes good sense," said Buchanan. But he was disquieted by Nora's silence. "Where do they stay?"

"Built a bunkhouse for 'em out on the plain," said Billy. "You know where the crick ran? Good half a day's ride out there. Them boys don't mix too good with the townspeople y' know."

"They come in for supplies?"

"Nope. That's my job, truckin' out. Some of 'em got wives—well, women— out there in cabins I built for 'em."

"And they stay away from Encinal?"

"Yep. When they want, they go home, over the border."

"I see." He saw that Billy had unconsciously built a tiny empire on the high plain. The townfolks would naturally resent this. Billy was a character always, from the time he was a boy. Headstrong was a mild word for him, Buchanan knew.

Teresa called and they went inside to a huge supper of beef and vegetables from the garden and apple pie and all the fixings. It was the best time of Buchanan's day.

He kept looking at Nora. There were faint circles beneath her eyes. He had learned to love the girl with all his heart, and now he worried. He decided to see

Avery after dinner; he wanted to know more about what went on in Encinal.

The Averys lived close to the stamp mill and assay office. Buchanan nursed a cup of after-dinner coffee and listened to the serious-minded man of the house.

"The mines are payin' off. No Golcondas, mind you, but nice and steady. Business is pretty good. The hotel is too big—bit off more 'n she could chew, the gal, Miss Beaumont. The marshal, he ain't much, and there's a fella works the desk and such, Freddy Daggett, and then there's the deputy, Rack Dolan. They're all tryin' to live off the hotel, saloon, and gamblin'. Hamilton Mizer at the bank has got a mortgage on it all, and he'd foreclose on his grandmother, that one."

"That about takes care of that crew," said Buchanan. "Now, about Billy."

"He spends more time—and money—around the hotel than anybody else in town."

Mrs. Avery came into the room,

sniffing, a plain lady with a pronounced chin. "Billy Button! Never see him in church. She brings in the baby. Not him. Out ganderin' around town, mainly at the hotel, or out ridin' with his cowboys from Mexico. I swan, Mr. Buchanan, he's turnin' into a bad one again. Like when he was little."

Avery said, "Now, Maw. It ain't all that bad. Billy doesn't mean any harm. That we know."

"He means to be like Mr. Buchanan," she said grimly. "Footloose and fancy free."

"Now, Maw—"

"No harm meant. But he's got the money, and Nora, she's tied up with the baby and Billy's got the itch. Don't tell me no, I can see it," she said defiantly. "Big notions. Too big for his britches."

"I wouldn't exactly say that," said her husband.

"Nora, she's the same gal. Never would sell the little house, you remember, Mr. Buchanan? Mousetrap's house? She keeps it clean and all. Don't even rent it. Takes

61

the baby down there and sets a lot when Billy's away."

"I hear we're to have a christenin'," Buchanan said. "Should be a real nice affair."

"Affair? Affair? We don't call it anything like that when a child is consecrated to the Lord!"

"Excuse me," said Buchanan humbly. "It's just I ain't accustomed to such doin's."

"Nor is Billy Button! If it's right for my Uncle Tom, says he, then it's right for me."

Avery interrupted. "Now, Maw, that's 'nough. You let Buchanan make up his own mind about the way things are."

"No, I do thank you both for tellin' me some things I was right curious about," said Buchanan. He arose and found his hat. "I feel right responsible for Nora and Billy. They truly are like family to me. I came here thinkin' it was like a home. Not havin' a home of my own you see . . . I'll be moseyin' along."

The woman said, "You mark my

words, Billy Button will be at the hotel in a poker game. Nothin' can keep him away from that table. And . . . that woman."

"Maw!" said Avery. "That's no way to talk."

She sniffed. "Don't tell me how to talk. The Lord has spoken to me. And that Billy thinks he's a new Tom Buchanan, you can lay to that. Buchanan is his god, which is against everything a husband and father should be."

"Maw!" said Avery.

Buchanan held up his hand. "No, Ed. She's dead right. Anybody picks me for a model is way off the trail. I'll say good evenin', now. And thanks for clearin' the air, both of you. I'll try to figure how to play this. It's a new game to me, the kids and all."

Avery went to the front door with him. "Maw gets carried away," he apologized.

"Power to her," said Buchanan. "See you, Ed."

He walked on Main Street, noting the differences in the town. He carried no weapon, as was his habit. Lights were

63

thrown by the cantina, a cowboy saloon, and the Palace Hotel. Otherwise the street was in dark shadows, people were abed at this hour, in preparation for the hard work of the coming day, when sunup to sundown were the average hours.

Between the general store and the bank was an unlighted alley. As Buchanan came abreast of this he was aware of movement therein. He moved, first left, then right, with great speed and force, then directly toward anticipated ambush, always a strategy he favored.

A musical voice said, "Hola, Buchanan. Stop where you are, please."

The language was Spanish, and he recognized the low, dulcet tone from a time in the past. He remained stock still in the mouth of the alley, out of the reflected lights of the hotel and the saloons.

He said, "Hola, Emalita."

"There are guns across the street," she said. "Juju is somewhere with his bow and arrow."

He answered in the same language. "So many against one? You flatter me."

"Do not jest, Buchanan. Jo-san's honor has been diminished. That is not good."

"Is Jo-san also with you?"

"No. He sulks in the hills. I am to speak with you."

"Speak, then." He put thumbs in his belt and waited. He could not see the Apaches, but he knew they were watching and ready to kill him. He could make out Emalita now in the shadow, a Mexican woman who had been taken prisoner but had never been a slave. Juju had claimed her and she had fall in love with the Apache chieftain. She was not handsome, but her face was strong and calm in her middle years. Jo-san was her only son, and Buchanan, facing her, knew his danger.

She said, "You sent a message."

"Yes. Rather than kill your son, I sent a warning."

"What good is it now? We could leave you dead where you stand."

"True," said Buchanan. "Therefore,

do so or keep on talking. But make your intention clear."

She said, "Ah, yes. Buchanan. A brave man. You have been a friend."

"When a friend is needed, a man does what he must." He knew better than to ask for favors, to plead the past. The Apache lived in the present.

She said, "The Indian agent is again a thief. The cattle they give us is scrawny, the grain rotten with worms. It has happened before. Now we are hungry."

"So you are off the reservation."

"Yes. And we have need of food."

"And guns." The musket in the hands of Jo-san had been a miserable weapon.

"We will not talk of guns," she said. "First, we need food. You warned against harming Mr. Billy Button. And you humiliated my son."

"I could've killed him and saved his honor," Buchanan pointed out.

"You know the difference." She spoke in harsh tones. "Now we throw your words back at you. Billy Button must pay. Cattle, money."

"That's bad talk, Emalita."

"Is it? Then let it be. We are desperate. If we are not paid, we will move."

"Against Billy's *vaqueros*? You will be in great danger, I think."

"Against Billy Button, who has everything, who hires *vaqueros* to shoot Apaches," she said, her voice growing harder with every word. "Against his wife and baby."

Buchanan drew a deep breath, controlling his speech. "So that's it."

"That is it," she said.

To her, to the Apaches, it was not at all complicated, he knew. Jo-san had been offended. Juju had not quite dared raid the herd on the high plain because of the *vaqueros* under Mando. Buchanan had come along at the right time, someone to whom they could talk, who understood them and their values and their customs —and who appreciated the danger of ignoring them.

He said, "You know me. If you harm the young ones you will have to kill me, too."

"Yes," she said simply.

"That will not be easy."

"No," she answered.

"But you are willing to try? You must indeed be hungry," he said.

"Our people are hungry. Jo-san is hungry for revenge."

Buchanan said slowly, "I will see what can be done."

"You will do!"

"Food," he agreed. "Probably beef. No guns, no bullets, Emalita."

"That is as may be." She could be devious. She was the only woman in history who spoke for the Apache. She was in herself a leader, with Juju backing her, with the tribe in awe of her. "You will signal us in the old way?"

"Can't remember all that smoke stuff," Buchanan said. "Give me time. Send a messenger. Let it be peaceable. And the Buttons, stay away from them. I won't have Nora and the baby choused by anybody. You understand?"

She laughed without humor. "I understand too much. You have a weak spot now, Buchanan. Never before. Now it is the baby and its mother. I understand that, believe me!"

She backed a step or two and was gone. She had kept her figure well for a woman of her age, he thought. She was a ruler by way of her hold on Juju, himself a strong man, and because of her brains and eloquence. She was a most dangerous person.

He waited a moment. No one saw or heard the Indians as they departed. No one had seen them arrive. They were ghosts in the night. If there were more of them, enough of them, the white man would never have been able to settle in the Southwest. Mangus Colorado had been a Mescalero and for years he had laid waste the region all because of the injustice of a renegade named Johnson and the continuing influx of white men avid of copper from the Santa Rita mine. Juju was a true Mescalero and Emalita was his alter ego.

Jo-san, of course, had been unfortunate with the musket. There was no way of gauging Jo-san's worth. He was small and thin, but so was Billy Button. They were of an age, it occurred to Buchanan: the waif who had become wealthy and the halfbreed who had nothing.

There was trouble ahead and Buchanan would be in the middle again. One more pleasant vacation among friends was in the process of being ruined, he thought. He entered the Palace Hotel in a bad frame of mind.

He paused in the small lobby listening to the sound coming from the saloon in back: the whirr of the wheel, the slap of cards, the click of chips. Behind the desk was a sleepy-eyed youth with a cowlick, who did not in any way resemble the figure of Freddy Daggett given by Coco in their private conversation regarding the hotel and its denizens.

He stood for a moment in the door to the bar and gaming room. Billy Button had not remained at home with his wife and baby and Coco Bean. He sat in a poker game, hat tilted, cigar in his mouth. Elton Beaumont, Rack Dolan, and the slick-haired Daggett were the other players. On a high dealer's chair overlooking the action, tiny feet tucked demurely beneath her long skirt, sat a little lady who could be none other than Heloise Beaumont. When her attention focused upon Buchanan, people turned and stared. Every eye was upon him as he moved across the room to the poker table.

Billy waved an arm. "Drinks are on me. Heloise, everybody, this here's my Uncle Tom Buchanan come to visit. This here's a celebration."

If there were any who recognized his name they did not so acknowledge. They accepted the drinks brought to them by a hard-faced bartender called Griff. They accepted Buchanan with a shrug, estimating his bulk but noting that he did not carry a six-shooter.

Billy went on. "Set down, Uncle Tom. This here's a house game, but it's the only one goin' right now. There's Dolan, Rack Dolan. And Daggett. And you know the marshal."

The lady slid down from the chair, displaying perfectly turned ankles and a wide, welcoming smile. She said, "Of course, Mr. Buchanan. May I join you, gentlemen?"

"It's your saloon," muttered Beaumont, unsmiling.

Billy said, "Uh-oh. There goes my luck. She beats me, Uncle Tom. She's the one took me for two thousand last week. Look out for her."

Buchanan tipped his hat to the back of his head, grinning. "Why, I always look out for pretty ladies. They're my favorite people to look out for."

She touched his arm as she took the chair between him and Billy Button. "Lawsy me, you do have the South in your mouth. Where from, sir?"

"East Texas, ma'am. Near the Louisiana line. Mom was from Geo'gia. Pa was Scottish."

"There, you see? I know a Southern gentleman when I see him." She patted Buchanan's hand but her eyes were upon Billy, her smile directed at him. And

Buchanan detected a touch of the fatuous in Billy's return grin.

There was something here that drew immediate attention. Beaumont wore a perpetual sneer. Freddy Daggett's eyes glinted in detached amusement. Rack Dolan held the cards in hands that were practiced.

Three women, Buchanan thought. Nora, Emalita, Heloise Beaumont. The West was hard on most women, but these had adjusted, one way or another, to their surroundings. Each had great strength, and two of them were dangerous. And the main target was Billy Button, who was totally ignorant of their intentions.

Heloise said, "Ten dollar ante against table stakes, Mr. Buchanan. Is that all right with you, suh?"

"High game," he commented.

"Dolan's deal," she chatted on. "Dealer's choice, of course, like all the Western games. I've learned a heap about the West, Mr. Buchanan."

"I bet you have," he said.

Dolan's voice was a croak. "Five card

stud." He dealt the hand around, to Daggett, Billy, Buchanan, Heloise Beaumont, then himself. Buchanan watched sleepy-eyed but intent. There was no crooked move in a gambling house that he had not mastered during his long friendship with the master, Luke Short. There were few he could not duplicate. The house man's deal was honest. Maybe they had taken Billy's two thousand on luck alone. And maybe they hadn't, he thought. Most likely they hadn't.

His first up card was an ace. He did not look at his hole card, watching the others in the game. Heloise showed a king, Billy a ten, Daggett and Dolan a trey and a deuce, which they folded as Buchanan bet ten dollars. Beaumont played along with Heloise and Billy.

The cards came again: a nine to Billy, a jack to Buchanan, an eight to Heloise, a king to Beaumont.

Heloise pouted, "There goes mah pair of kings!"

Buchanan said, "A real shame. Makes

my ace look better now, don't it?" He bet twenty dollars.

Billy said, "I stay. I got to stay."

Beaumont met the bet. Heloise hesitated, very ladylike, tentative, eyebrows drawn in perplexity. Then she put in twenty dollars with a sigh.

Buchanan figured out the odds. Billy had two spades showing in succession. Beaumont might have an ace in the hole, which would make him high man. As for the lady, he figured kings backed up or a pair of eights; surely she was putting on a show.

"Cards," said Dolan, and distributed them. Billy drew another spade, a three-spot. Heloise got another eight to pair her. Buchanan looked at a queen and Beaumont grunted over a four of diamonds.

It was time to edge the hole card. Buchanan peeked, covering it with his huge palm. He saw the corner of the ace of spades without changing expression one iota.

The woman was high with the pair of

eights. She said, "Well now, that's real nice. But look at all those high cards showin'! Lawsy me, I check."

Buchanan pushed in money. "I got to bet fifty to see who's got 'em."

"Beats me," said Billy cheerfully. He turned his cards down. Beaumont hesitated, then shrugged and did likewise.

Heloise said, "Just little old me? Goodness sake!" She made a business of studying her hole card. Then she said brightly, "I raise two hundred dollars!"

Buchanan leaned back in his chair. Three eights, he thought. Maybe they had snookered her an eight on the first card and then she had been the recipient of another pair by a trick he did not know. Maybe they were too smart for him. It was time to find out.

"Call." He pushed in the two hundred, and now his eyes were openly upon Dolan as the house man dealt. There was silence in the room. The card came to Buchanan. It was the ace of diamonds. He caught the intake of breath from the woman beside him. Her card proved to be the ten of diamonds.

Buchanan said, "I tap you, my dear," and shoved all his money into the pot.

She said, "Oh, no. No, you don't, suh! Three aces beats me. One thing I know. I know when I'm beat."

Buchanan raked in the pot. There had been a ring of truth in her voice that somewhat surprised him. She was smiling now as though she had not been in the pot at all, had not lost a nickel. Whatever had gone on, whether it was honest or not, she was accepting defeat without wincing. The others were also poker-faced, although according to Billy and to Ed Avery, they were allied in a common cause. These were no ordinary people, he decided. If they had a plot it would be a deep one.

And between them and Juju and his Emalita were Billy Button and his family. Including the little baby, less than a year old. It was a loaded situation and Buchanan did not like it.

The game went along in desultory

fashion. Evidently they had figured Buchanan was onto any trick and were taking it easy. Billy lost and talked a lot. Heloise remained bright and perky, holding her own as Dolan played them to his vest like a good house man. Daggett won and lost, and Buchanan steadily won small pots, having a lucky evening.

It became Buchanan's deal and he called for a round of straight poker, Western style, open on anything. There had been one small peculiarity that had bothered him all evening: Neither Billy nor he had been successful at winning a hand of draw poker. He could swear that no one had dealt bottoms or seconds. He knew the cards were not marked. He was ahead of the game and had been since the first pot, yet there was something in the air, something hovering, waiting to descend upon this poker table.

He dealt to Heloise, to Beaumont, to Dolan, to Daggett, and to Billy, five cards each. He held his own cards lightly, his hat brim pulled low, redoubling his attention to each, trying to keep them all in focus.

The lady said, "I open for ten."

They all played in this pot. Buchanan edged his cards. He had a pair of aces—they had been with him all night, responsible for his winnings; lucky bullets, he thought.

He caught Dolan's questioning gaze—and in a flash realized it was not directed at him but slightly behind him.

He did not turn his head or change expression. He had checked out the bar mirror immediately on sitting down and knew the sharpest eyes could not pick up a reflection of his cards in it.

"Cards if any."

They signaled for the draw: one card to Heloise, one to Beaumont, three to Dolan, two to Daggett, three to Buchanan. Then he flicked a chip on the floor, apologized, bent to retrieve it.

Griff, the bartender, was making a move with his right hand. Buchanan noted a square frame on the back bar. In that frame there had to be a magnifying glass. Griff could maneuver it at will. Dolan, Daggett, and Beaumont could see into it. Heloise, Buchanan, and Billy could not.

Thus, if they were lucky, or the players in the mirror's field of vision were careless, the hands could be read and bets made accordingly. Signals to Heloise to stay in a hand or drop out could be casual, undetectable. It was an old wrinkle, boldly managed.

He said, "Your bet, I believe, Miss Heloise."

Billy was looking at his hand. Buchanan's was under his fist where no one could see it. She hesitated. Dolan turned his cards face down and tapped them.

She said, "I bet two hundred dollars."

She had filled something with her one-card buy, Buchanan thought, a straight, a flush, a full house . . . she might even have fours or a straight flush to push it to the limit. If she did, it was pure luck and Buchanan did not believe in that kind of luck very often.

Beaumont said, "I can't see that."

Dolan and Daggett dropped and Billy, twisting in his seat, put down his cigar. Now Dolan could read Billy's hand, Buchanan thought. The kid was careless under stress.

Billy said, "I raise another two hundred."

Buchanan had to look at his hand. One by one he slipped the pips into view, hand against his vest, his shoulders blocking out the mirror behind him. He saw Dolan lean to the right, trying to get an angle as the bartender manipulated the magnifying mirror. He also saw that he had drawn three kings.

He said, "Raise five hundred."

Heloise was staring at Dolan, who was looking at the ceiling. Beaumont had craned to look at the bar. Now he turned back, his mustache drooping.

Heloise said faintly, "I do declare. You are really a big, bad man, Mr. Buchanan. I call."

"Call," said Billy. "I call, too."

Buchanan laid down his aces, then his three kings. The air hissed from the lungs of Heloise. She managed to maintain composure but she was badly hurt, Buchanan knew. She smiled weakly at Billy, who flipped his cards to the center of the table, blurting, "No chance of beatin' Uncle Tom tonight. I swan to ginney, he's got all the luck."

"True," said Buchanan. He stacked chips with skill and dispatch. "And now cash me in, please."

"Already?" asked the lady. "You're not giving us a chance to come back."

Buchanan waited until Dolan had reluctantly paid him the value of the chips. Then he arose and stretched, smiled down at the lady.

"I'll say this. Your game is almost honest."

Everyone in the room gasped. Heloise turned pale. Beaumont jerked back in his chair, Dolan's hand went to his belt. Only Daggett sat slumped, eyes bright, waiting and watching.

"I beg your pardon, suh. You insult me?"

Buchanan turned and made a big,

catlike leap. Just as Griff was putting the mirror away his hand closed upon it. He held it up for all to see.

"If your back's to this thingamajig, look out, gents. They can read it fine if it's managed right. Just a small cheat, enough to give 'em a big edge."

Heloise exclaimed, "Well, I never! Dolan! Griff! You are fired. You hear me? Fired. This instant. Why, I ought to have Elton arrest you and put you in the jail, I truly should."

Griff was taking off his apron. Dolan shoved back his chair, still expressionless.

Beaumont said, "There's a stage out in the mornin'. You two be on it. I swear, this is a disgrace to Encinal."

"Uh-huh," said Buchanan. "It sure is, ain't it?"

"It's a reflection on poor me." There were actually tears in her eyes.

"I ought to throw you men in jail!" Beaumont said. "You get out right this minute, you heah?"

They were already leaving. Heloise faced Buchanan.

"If you feel we owe you anything, suh. I mean, what can I say? They were our hired hands."

"Just forget it," Buchanan said. "One of those things that do happen, ma'am. Billy, want to call it a night?"

"Yeah." Billy's cigar had gone out. When Heloise appealed to him with round eyes he smiled weakly. They went out onto the street and began the walk toward home.

After a while Billy said, "She knowed about it."

"Certain," said Buchanan.

"Damn. They were playin' me for a sucker."

"Uh-huh."

"I'll run 'em outa town. I'll—"

"You'll lay low. You'll act like she didn't know."

"I won't do no such of a thing!"

"You'd better, young fella," Buchanan told him. "You better be ready for a heap of trouble. You and me, we better start usin' our heads to figure what's goin' to happen."

84

"I don't get it."

"Well, let's start with how I come here thinkin' all is lovey-dovey with you and Nora, everything nice and smooth and fine."

"It's fine. Nora's got the baby. I like a little fun. I got the herd. What's so wrong?"

"I'll let you think about that. Now, there's Juju, he's hungry. I had to upset his boy Jo-san, for which I am now sorry. So I got to take care of that. And you got to watch out for the Apaches and for whatever that little lady's got planned. And maybe Coco's got to fight their man to learn about that."

"About what?"

"Billy," said Buchanan, "when you been around like I have, you begin to smell things. Like that Heloise and her brother, if he is her brother. And Daggett and the big fella, McMillan. And Dolan, I'd bet. They travel in a gang, son. They are what you call con people. They work confidence games. With the fighter, with one thing and another. And they are very smart people, very smart."

"But she put up cash to build the hotel."

"Which would be a great front for them. But somethin' went wrong, the hotel ain't payin' off. Which leads me to believe they got plans. And when they want to fight Coco, I know they got some kind of a scheme."

Billy walked a few steps, then asked, "Juju is goin' after my stock? Heloise and them after my money?"

"That's about the way it is. Y' see, Billy, when you get to be a big, rich man people go after you. They want a share." Buchanan laughed. "It's natural enough. Thing is, we're here, we're onto them. We feed Juju maybe . . . a little bit. We watch them others."

"I been a damn fool," said Billy.

"Sure. Who ain't, one time or another?" Buchanan touched his shoulder. "Let's go home and you be specially nice to Nora, huh? That'll be a good start."

They went the rest of the way without further words. Billy's head hung low, his thoughts turned inward. It was, Buchanan thought, a pretty good start at that.

3

EMALITA sat cross-legged, carefully away from the men of the little band. Juju was talking and always she maintained her place as a squaw in order to save face. Her mind, however, functioned freely, listening, silently criticizing. There were six young braves and six older men and she was the only woman. Plus Jo-san, that is, her son. She regarded him with puzzlement.

He was more Apache than Mexican, which was natural enough since he had been raised in the Mescalero tradition. But she would have wished some of herself in him, especially now.

Juju was saying, "Buchanan will see that we get meat."

"How do we know?" Jo-san persisted.

"Because he has given his word."

"The word of a white-eye!"

"Nevertheless, we know Buchanan."

"Then you know nothing!"

Juju looked at his son with the eyes of a snake. There were times when Emalita thought father would kill son. There was feeling between them; it was never good with them.

There was another young one called Juan Who Runs, nicknamed Moose because he was the biggest Apache in the mountains. He was not strong in the head, and he followed Jo-san in everything. Few cared to debate with Jo-san because Moose was always ready to take up the fight for his smaller, skinnier friend. Moose was stupid, Emalita knew.

Juju said bluntly, "Young men are fools, which is forgivable. But when young men have big mouths it is unforgivable."

"We fools are starving for meat. The skinny birds, the herbs and roots, is this food for men? The white-eyes drove all the game from the hills. The agent cheats us. And you would trust this Buchanan?"

"I will give him time," said Juju. He had agreed upon this with Emalita. He could see trouble coming, for he was a true leader with great spirit. But he would not go against both Emalita and Buchanan. "That is enough. We will speak on it no more."

It was very early in the morning, before the sun had got above the eastern horizon. The young braves had asked for the meeting. They now moved apart from the older men. Juju remained where he was, squatting beside the fire. Emalita came out with a bowl of gruel in her hands and squatted close, serving him, using this as an excuse to speak to him.

She whispered, "Jo-san and the others will go out."

"Yes," said her husband.

"They may be killed."

"Yes."

"Yet we cannot stop them."

"It is a matter for the wind and the sky and the stars."

"They will go for the cattle, the fat beef in the graze of Billy Button."

"You know that much, woman?"

"It is a matter of common sense," she said.

He nodded "Yes. They will go, as you say. Six of them and Jo-san. Tell me, woman, how many will return?"

"That I do not know. But not all of them will return."

"And the beef?"

"Better we should wait for Buchanan to make good his promise."

"And if he does not?"

"We take the girl and her baby."

"You would do that?"

She said, "Our people must eat."

"You would dare Buchanan?"

She said, "To eat, we must dare the world."

"Yes, and you will be there, with the warriors."

"Am I not always there?"

"You are. But your son—I fear for your son."

"*Our* son," she said. "I too fear for him. May the gods protect him. He has lost some of his spirit to Buchanan."

"He could regain it by counting coup,

like the cousins from the plains. Or in any other way—after we receive the meat Buchanan promised."

She sighed, a mother always, even in these surroundings, under this pressure. "He will not listen to us. The young get more headstrong every day."

"They should be whipped. We do not punish them enough."

"Perhaps," she agreed. "But it is not the time."

"No, it is not the time. They may die, but we may not punish them."

They watched Jo-san and Moose and the others. They had their heads together, they spoke in low tones. It was plain as day that they were planning to go against the dictates of Juju and the older men. Everyone in the camp knew it. This group was out on the raid, they were not among the elder tribesmen who would enforce discipline in their harsh way, according to tradition. Up here in the mountains they could only be held in line by violence—by killing the leader or leaders. Juju and Emalita could not do this.

The sun had begun to brighten the hills when Buchanan kissed Nora and the baby and left them in the care of Coco and the pretty Mexican girl named Teresa. Billy was already saddling up a grulla he fancied when Nightshade neighed greeting and was ready to go.

Billy said, "I got a bull that will knock your eyes out, Uncle Tom. I got blooded stock out there. I'm buildin' for the future of the breed."

"Big words." Buchanan laughed. "Haven't you got a few stray head which ain't all that proud of ancestry?"

"Well, maybe a few. Why?"

"Juju's people are hungry," said Buchanan. "Might save a heap of trouble if I toted them some beef."

"Juju? You wanta give him meat? Uncle Tom, you know how those renegades are. They damn near killed us once, remember?"

"They might damn near do it again,"

Buchanan told him. He hesitated, then added, "You got to think of Nora and the baby."

Billy stared at him. "You know somethin', Uncle Tom?"

"I know somethin'."

"Well . . . I dunno. Let me think about it. Let me talk to Mando and them. The *vaqueros* are mighty proud that no Apache dares raid 'em. The cattle—it's like they owned 'em."

"They have pride and that's good. To be stubborn, that's plain stupid. Why invite a fight? Someone's bound to be hurt."

"You always was peaceable," Billy said. "I see what you mean. Maybe givin' em a few head would save fightin' and dyin'—but maybe it would give 'em ideas. Maybe they'll think we're soft."

"Juju has known me a few years. He don't think I'm soft," Buchanan said. "His wife, Emalita, she don't think I'm soft. But they ain't scared of me nor anybody else, neither. These ain't the renegades you knew, Billy."

"They're Apaches. I don't trust 'em, not no way."

"Uh-huh," said Buchanan. It was no use to talk further at this time, he saw. Billy was headstrong always. Mando was about Billy's age, he was a foreman, he would have his pride also. It did not shape up well. Buchanan put the saddle on Nightshade and rode out to the high plain and the cattle of which Billy was so proud. Pride, pride, what was the saying? *Pride goeth before a fall*, he thought, that was it.

He could, at any rate, enjoy the countryside. This was his favorite hunting and fishing country. The higher they rode the better he felt. The clouds rode the tops of the mountains and the sun reflected all the colors of the rainbow, and for that small time every prospect was pleasing.

Billy was silent as they rode. The elegance of saguaro did not attract his notice, the wail of a mother cougar from the rocks drew no comment from him.

Buchanan communed with nature in silence for miles.

Then Billy blurted, "You think she's a crook? A real crook?"

"I do. First place, she ain't Southern."

"How do you know that?"

"Because I once was my own self. Now you take that Beaumont. He is a Confederate all right. So's Daggett but he went north to school some place. Maybe Princeton in New Jersey; lots of 'em go up there. Old school, Aaron Burr was president of it one time."

"You can be sure of all that about them people?"

"When you been listenin' to folks as long as me you'll be able to know somethin' about where they're from. This here is a big country, people talk different hither and thither."

"I just plumb hate to think of her bein' a crook," Billy confessed. "She's been so doggone nice to me. Not . . . not what people might think, neither. Just . . . friendly."

"Uh-huh. Real friendly with your money."

"That's my own business. A fella needs some fun. Nora's got the baby. Her and Teresa are always makin' over him."

"Seen it before," Buchanan said. "Jealousy."

"Jealous? Of my own kid?"

"Yep."

The silence fell again. The clouds changed form a dozen times. Buchanan took it all in; there was nothing in the great country that escaped his notice, then nor at any other time. He was a frontiersman, one of a breed. He had come here early and he would, he hoped, die here with the wind blowing and the sun shining and the clouds playing clown to him in the heavens.

Billy said, as they came within hailing distance of the grama grass of the high plain, "You never had a kid of your own, did you, Uncle Tom?"

"Nope."

"Okay." He said no more, but the

doubt, the rebellion was there, between them.

Buchanan kept his own counsel. The bunkhouse was at the edge of a wooded section; the graze spread far to the south, east, and west of it. There was a big corral and a small barn where ailing animals could be sheltered from the weather when necessary. There were cabins up and down a road, which had been worn by men and the hooves of horses. It was more than ample, it was up to date in every possible fashion.

There was an office at the south side of the bunkhouse over which a crudely lettered sign said: FOREMAN—COME ON IN EVERYWUN.

As Buchanan and Billy dismounted, a husky young man came out of the office and rushed to greet them, both hands outstretched. It was Mando, taller, heavier, weather-worn, sporting a *bandido* mustache. The boy from the old hotel had grown up.

"Hoy. I expected," Mando said. "We kill a steer, we break out flour and peaches, no? Salome, she make a pie. Whiskey a plenty. Julio plays the mandolin for my boss and my old, great friend, Thomas Buchanan."

Billy said, "That's what the doctor ordered. How's everything goin' up here?"

"Good. Excellent. Very well." His eyes flickered. "But Julio says he saw Injun sign."

"Juju is out, didn't you know that?" Billy said, scowling.

"I did not know but I suspect," said Mando. "That is why you don't see no *vaqueros* around here, no?"

"You got 'em out scoutin'?"

"Guarding the herd. And the bool, no?"

Buchanan said in Spanish, "Mando, I see you're wearing the fancy. How come?"

Mando touched the red sash around his waist with pride, took a step so that the jingle-bob spurs sounded their merry tune, winked. His hat was oversized, trimmed with tassels. Even his Colt was

99

bright with silver plate. "Billy, he likes it this way."

Billy flushed. "They look good," he said defensively. "I pay for the duds. They get 'em over the border. If we got Mex *vaqueros*, why not let 'em dress right?"

"No reason," said Buchanan. "Unless they wore chaps up here where's there ain't any brush. Then it'd be plain silly."

Mando giggled. "Hola! See what I told you, Billy?"

"Well, we quit the chaps, didn't we?" Billy was not entirely happy. "You want to ride the range, Uncle Tom? Look over the herd and all?"

Buchanan said, "That'll be fine. After we eat, huh?"

"Oh, yeah. I forgot. You are always hungry. Got some grub for now, Mando?"

"You betcha."

The kitchen was a wing of the bunkhouse, and there was a dining hall with a long, trestle table. They sat at one end and the stout, middle-aged cook called

Salome came smiling, bringing ham and corn bread and cold beans and canned apricots. Buchanan ate enormously, enjoying every bite. It was ranch food and he loved it.

Billy said as they drank coffee strong enough to walk in from the kitchen by itself, "Good thing we didn't get Coco into boxin' with Mac, huh? They must've had somethin' figured for that."

Buchanan said, "Yep. They had somethin' goin', all right. No question about it. Only one thing."

"What's that?"

"Nobody, and specially dudes and Southerns, got an idea what a terrific fighter Coco is."

"Well, sure. But if it was fixed—crooked some way—he wouldn't have a chance."

"No matter. It didn't happen. Seems like I could have another small dish of the apricots. Got a bit of an empty spot in me, right here."

Salome was a happy dark lady, bringing

fresh baked bread to go with the fruit. Buchanan ate.

Nora put on a dress sent from Denver and twirled around, the tips of her shiny black shoes twinkling. "How do you like it? Never got to wear it before."

Teresa clapped her hands. Coco grinned to show his gold tooth, the baby cooed in his arms.

"Mighty fine," Coco said. "You makin' me proud to walk to town."

Teresa said, "My lady, she is always pretty, no?"

"Yes," said Coco. "So let's take her to the stores."

Teresa held her arms out but the baby squawked and clung to Coco. Nora laughed.

"You lost a child, there, Teresa."

"He'll be sorry some day." But Teresa was unperturbed as the trio left the big house and walked slowly down the hill to Encinal.

Coco felt fine. His new clothes shone in the sunlight, his pocket was lined with fresh, green money, and these dear people had greeted him with true warmth. He asked for little, and the immediate kindness of Nora and Billy and Teresa and the attachment of the baby filled him with pleasure.

They went into the general store. In the grocery department Nora filled the string bags they had brought, and Coco insisted on slinging them over the shoulder not occupied with the baby. They walked down the street and were in front of the bank when Heloise Beaumont seemed to materialize out of the boardwalk in their path, all smiles, beaming upon the baby, touching it with her surprisingly strong little hands.

Jim McMillan stood behind her, his eyes fixed upon Coco. He was a huge tiger of a man, his mien challenging.

Heloise said, "Oh, here comes brother Elton. He'll want to see how much little Billy has grown."

"His name is Thomas Mulligan," said Nora too sweetly. "For Mr. Buchanan and my grandfather."

"Ah, yes. I always forget . . . Elton!"

He was wearing a gray coat two shades lighter than his gray, striped trousers. He bowed to Nora, ignoring Teresa and Coco, made baby talk at Thomas Mulligan.

McMillan said in the background, "I guess you're still scared to fight me, huh, nigger?"

Coco showed his gold tooth. "Nope."

"You ain't agreein' to do so, though."

Heloise said, "Now, Mac. This is Mr. Buchanan's nigra. It's not proper to address him on the street in this fashion."

Nora's eyes began to sparkle. "Coco is *not* Mr. Buchanan's anything. He is a free man and a champion!"

Coco interposed, still grinning. "Don't matter what they think or what they say, Miss Nora. They *Southe'n*."

It was an insult if they cared to take it that way. Heloise actually smiled. McMillan looked confused. But Beaumont stiffened and glared.

"And what is wrong with being from the South?" he demanded, then bit his lip, believing that he had descended to the level of the black man in asking the question.

Coco said mildly, "Not anything, Mister, unless you take it wrong."

McMillan butted in. "North, south, I don't give a care. I want to fight this fella for a purse. Black, white, pink, blue, I can whip him."

Coco said, "Shoot, lots of people think they can whup me. That is until I hit 'em once."

"No use, Mac," Beaumont said superciliously. "You can't talk sense to 'em, you know. Black people have no true brain."

Heloise slapped her hands together. "Now, I will not heah this! Yawl are bein' rude to Miz Button."

"I do beg youah pardon, Miz Button," Beaumont said, bowing deeply. "But what I say is well known in the South. Niggers are like animals."

"And you are insulting my friend!" Nora flared. "He could beat you to a pulp with one hand!"

"True. They have enormous strength," said Beaumont. "But then, so do horses."

"He can't beat me to a pulp," McMilllan crowed. "He can't beat one side of me. For all the money in Encinal, he can't beat me."

Nora's ears began to burn. The prune face of Hamilton Mizer came poking from the door of the bank. His nose wrinkled at Coco. He was no kinder toward the others, but the word "money" was in the air and people were beginning to congregate. A dozen citizens gathered, listening, staring.

Nora said, "This is too much. Let's go home, Coco . . . Teresa. Please!"

McMillan said, "That's right. Run home, nigger."

Coco still smiled but a bead of sweat was on his brow. He turned, the string bags still dangling, the baby in his arms. Teresa, not smiling, her eyes flashing, came close and said, "Let me take him. It is shameful you should be carrying everything."

He said, "No disgrace in totin' for

106

friends." But because his hands were sweating he let her take Thomas Mulligan. He walked straight into the ring of spectators, Nora and Teresa at his heels. Heloise promptly fell into line, staring down anyone who came close.

She said, "You are absolutely right, honey. I do declare, my own brother disgraces me in public!"

Nora said, "If Uncle Tom was here they wouldn't dare."

"You are purely right! Mr. Buchanan is a wonderful man. Smart as a whip. He proved two of my employees to be dishonest, did you know?"

"I heard," Nora said, trying to maintain neutrality in the face of Heloise's kindness.

"I am really grateful! Oh, dear, here they are again! Elton, you must not!"

Beaumont gestured with the hat he still held in his hand. "Ladies, I wish to apologize. Mac, here, he now realizes his error. Mac!"

McMillan said, "I'm sorry, ladies, I really am."

Nora snapped, "You should apologize to Coco, not to us."

McMillan turned, towering over Coco. "I shouldn't have called names. I take it back."

Coco said, "It don't make no never mind."

Beaumont said, "I just spoke to Mr. Mizer. He very much wants the boxing match to take place."

"And who cares about him?" Nora demanded.

"Well, he is the town's leading citizen, in a way," Beaumont said. "And he suggests the town would benefit by the match."

"The town?" Heloise tapped her pearly teeth with an index finger. She looked doubtfully at Nora. "It is our responsibility, I suppose. Isn't it?"

Nora said hesitantly, "In a way . . . but I don't think it wise to agree to anything without a lot of thought."

"Of course not," said Heloise. "Hard thought. And, well . . . boxing is not a matter for ladies, now, is it?"

"I'm not that kind of a lady," Nora said bluntly. "If a boxing match would help the town and Uncle Tom and Coco were agreeable, I would be for it."

Beaumont cried, "Gallantly said, Miz Button. You are indeed a lady of spirit."

"Wonderful!" Heloise said, shining with admiration. "I shall join you! Together we shall make this a success!"

"But I'm not sure it can be done," Nora said.

"Mr. Mizer said that the bank will match every dollar put up by the townspeople," Beaumont announced. "I have given him fifty dollars as a starter."

"Me, I put up a hundred," said McMillan. "You, Bean, you got a hundred dollars?"

Coco grinned again. "I got plenty money. If'n you put it up, I can put it up and more besides!"

"Now, Coco," Nora began, then desisted. It was a matter of pride with Coco, she saw. He had taken their insults, now he could even the score.

McMillan said, "I'd like to see you do

that, Bean." Coco turned around. Nora called after him, Teresa cuddled the baby and walked swiftly toward home. Coco came to the bank, looked at Hamilton Mizer, reached into his pocket. Nora hustled down the street after Coco. Before she could arrive, he had thrust a sheaf of bills at the banker.

"This here's the money you stuck up your nose at. I know how much is there —over two thousand dollars. You people talkin' big. You match it. Then I'll whup your big-mouth man for you!"

Mizer seized the money. Nora brought up short, too late. Coco turned and faced the trailing citizens who were taking in all this with great pleasure.

"You people always puttin' down black. I don't see a black man or woman in this burg. So now, get up your money to match nigger money. If it helps your town, you can give thanks to a nigger."

He wheeled around, the string bags still swinging from his shoulder. Nora hesitated, then knew it was too late to mend matters. She followed him.

Heloise intercepted them. "I just think it's wonderful!" she cried. "Such a brave man to speak up for his kind! To put up his own money! Now Mr. Mizer and all of them will have to dig deep, won't they? I'm so glad you support the event, Miz Button!"

"Yes," said Nora weakly. "Yes, indeed."

They walked back up the hill to the house that Billy built. Nora was shaken to her heels. She had a huge hunch that Uncle Tom Buchanan would not approve of what had taken place. And she was not quite sure that she could explain it. The Beaumonts had confused her somewhat. She didn't understand it.

Buchanan rode the range. The cattle were sleek, and the bull called Big Boy was all that had been claimed about him. The *vaqueros* all rode fine cutting ponies and showed wide smiles and gleaming teeth and the handlebar mustache that seemed to be the height of style.

Julio, however, was old and bent-shouldered and his costume was a hickory shirt and overalls tucked into worn boots, which had once cost a hundred dollars when new. His hat curled up at the edges like Buchanan's Stetson. His horse was a canny dun, neither large nor small, and very swift in motion.

Buchanan said to him in Spanish, "How does it go, Julio?"

"I am uncle," Julio said, a grin cracking his walnut face. "Mando is my nephew. These children, they are very brave and they learn well."

"In time they will be good men if they work hard."

Julio shrugged. "Hard? Let us say they try, Señor Buchanan. It is not like in our time, you know that."

"Maybe it is better. We did not have it so good."

"True. Very true. But is it better?"

"You found the Apache tracks?"

"Juju. I know him."

"Yes. I have seen Emalita," Buchanan said.

"A woman, indeed." But he did not smile.

"They require food."

"Beef."

"Yes. The beef of Billy Button."

Julio waved toward the hills. "They are up yonder. They watch. And I watch."

"And your young men?"

"I, that is it. They do not properly read sign," Julio said sadly. "They are inclined to laugh at old folk."

"They had better be careful," Buchanan told him. "I have out a watch on Señora Button and the baby."

Julio scowled. "Emalita?"

"Yes. She is very smart."

"She will get her man killed and her son killed and maybe some others." Julio straightened the bent shoulders. "All our lives we have fought them, as you know. They have killed and captured thousands of us. Some day we will do to them as they have done to us!"

Buchanan shook his head. "They won't hold still long enough, Julio."

The shoulders drooped again. "You are

right. They melt into the mountains. Emalita, that she-devil, she gives them the benefit of her brains."

"Would you give them a few of the steers?"

Julio replied slowly, "I would, but my nephew would not. Nor will Boss Billy. The young men would make fun. Young men would rather fight than pay tribute."

"No tribute. Just food for hungry people," Buchanan said. "I advise it."

"And Boss Billy?"

"I don't know," Buchanan admitted.

"Then we must wait and see."

"If you wait too long, they will be down upon us. One way or another. Emalita and Juju would go after the baby and maybe the mother," Buchanan said. "Julio, what do you think?"

"Are the young of the Apache different from the young of the rancho?"

Buchanan shook his head. "I am a man of peace. I would avoid a fight. But the young people—well, I was young myself. It seems a long while ago but it's true."

"We must be ready," Julio said. "I will

give orders to drive the herd in close, especially the bull, no?"

"If they could chase 'em in for the celebration and if you could set a guard?"

Julio said, "I will not wait for orders, señor. I believe you are right."

Buchanan said, "*Hasta la vista*." He rode the perimeter of the graze that Billy had taken for himself and came back to the little settlement of cabins and bunkhouse. It was coming on dark when he had washed and made ready for the evening to which Billy seemed to look forward with immense gusto. Buchanan wore his gunbelt that night and outside the hall in a dark spot he hid his rifle and some ammunition.

The long table was set and Salome now had help. Women came from the cabins, four of them, not very young nor truly beautiful, but smiling and colorful in their gay raiment, women who were willing to spend part of the year out on the high plain away from civilization. Few if any were married to the young men, Buchanan surmised. One had a guitar, which she softly played as they sat down to a groaning board.

For a while Buchanan had no other thought than food and drink and the sound of the guitar and voices blending in lilting Latin melodies. It was a great pleasure, and he enjoyed it to the hilt.

Julio was absent. Mando went outside several times. Two riders came in, sullen, to a late dinner. These had been assigned the early guard. Two left to take their places, no happier than their fellows, taking a bottle of tequila with them.

Buchanan sat back. At the head of the table Billy had been doing more drinking than eating. Now he got up and danced his notion of a fandango with one of the women. All applauded, for Billy was the Patron. Salome came with a bottle of the good whiskey and poured a dollop in Buchanan's glass. She paused, staring at him, then whispered in his ear.

"Julio does not come in. Could it be something?"

Buchanan said, "It could be something."

"And Mando knows?"

"Mando guesses that perhaps, just maybe, mind you, his Uncle Julio may know that which is something."

She said, "Aiee. Gracias, señor."

He sipped his drink. The music had increased in tempo. A mandolin tinkled away, the guitar thrummed. They had one of the big sombreros now and were doing the hat dance. Buchanan had seen it done better in the cantinas below the border. Billy Button was not the greatest high stepper. The whiskey flowed like a small rivulet.

Buchanan went outside. In the heat of the excitement around the now-ruined hat, no one noticed. He drifted to where he had left the rifle and began a foot patrol. The herd—the prime beef and the bull, that is—had been driven into the near pasture. He thought he could discern the hunched shoulders of Julio aboard a pony. There was very little moon and the clouds drifted in a semibright sky.

It was a good night for it, Buchanan thought. On the other hand any person, friend or enemy, would be a target for the alert. He decided to move toward the hills. If they came at all they would have to come down the slopes. He knew their ways, the way of the mountain lion—or the snake. It was impossible to detect them at a distance.

Away from the bunkhouse and the cabins he walked a bit faster. It would be good to slough off the lethargy of the heavy food and drink even if nothing dangerous was afoot.

He was a mile away from the lights of the buildings when he knew they were out. He could not have told how he knew. It was in the air, partly an odor, partly a shimmering sense of their movement. He went down at once lest he provide them with a target.

They were not close enough. He could not see them, he could only feel them in that peculiar way. He began to crawl back the way he had come, angling, seeking the smallest brush, the meanest piñon into which he could weld his bulk, so that the shadow was complete, even though distorted. He moved quickly because he knew they would not want to give themselves away by firing a shot at him. He was aware of their bows and arrows, but he had survived so many of these thrusts of ill fortune that he had no real fear of them.

He had not located them when the first shot sounded. He heard their yell, then, and began to run. They were hitting directly at the herd; they must have scouted it well as the *vaqueros* drove it in. Now it was bunched and their task was easy.

The attack, he knew, was purely intended to do damage, to frighten the *vaqueros* and Billy into action, into providing the beef. Certainly they knew they would have no time to butcher the steers they brought down.

Buchanan ran faster than he believed he could. Julio was with the herd and possibly Billy would be running out with a gun, not being careful because it was not his nature to use caution.

There was a profile, an Indian larger

than the Apaches Buchanan had known. He was aiming an arrow, stretching the bow, a long one, heavy, powerful. Buchanan fired at him offhand, wishing not to kill, wishing this whole action was not taking place.

The tall Indian fell, his voice keening the death song. Buchanan's bullet had done its job better than he had intended. Now the Apaches were howling and their voices filled the night, terrible and fiendish. Buchanan fired again into the sounds.

Again there was a burst of fire. The sound of injured animals blended with the Indian yells. The *vaqueros* were turning out and the lead was flying.

Buchanan hit the ground and burrowed down. He was in danger from both sides now. The Apaches fled, as he knew they must; he heard them go by him not a hundred feet away. He did not shoot at them. Enough damage had been done, he thought. The moon appeared from behind a cloud, as though to view the fight, and he thought he saw Jo-san running, chin on shoulder, the rear guard of the little group. There were not more than half a dozen of them. Buchanan then understood—the young braves going out, Juju and Emalita and the others remaining in camp, disapproving.

Now it was time to worry about Encinal. For if the youths failed, then the wiser heads must prove that they were superior. And that meant danger to Nora and the baby.

He got up and walked over to where the *vaqueros* were huddled, around the dead body of the tall Indian. They were arguing about who might have slain him.

Julio was off to one side, standing over the motionless bulk of Big Boy, the bull. Julio was watching him die. Billy Button was cursing the Indians, the luck, everything in the world that came to his mind.

Julio looked at Buchanan. "Five steer. They shot good."

"Now it's a question of what to do with the meat," Buchanan said.

"Yes."

"They shot it. They should have it," Buchanan said.

Billy Button turned on him in red rage. "They killed my prize bull! You want me to give them the meat from him?"

"It's the smart thing to do."

"I'll see the whole damn Apache nation in hell first!"

"Uh-huh," said Buchanan. "And your bull will still be dead."

Buchanan went into the bunkhouse. He had not finished the drink poured for him by Salome. He drank it now and padded into the kitchen. The women were recovering from their fright. Salome was rallying them, ordering them to clean up the mess made by the party.

She looked at Buchanan, found the bottle, poured once more. "It was something," she said.

"Yes."

"Julio is alive. Mando is alive."

"Yes."

"But the bool is dead." She nodded. "It is a sign."

Buchanan sipped his drink. "You are Julio's woman?"

"I am Julio's wife," she said proudly. "I am not as the others here. I am paid to run this kitchen, not for anything else."

"Uh-huh," said Buchanan. "Let me tell you, if it wasn't for Julio, there'd be dead people here. So while I am gone, bid him beware."

"*Sí*, señor, he will beware. And now the other men will beware, because they will have fear."

"And the meat will be stripped and hung."

"As always. We have the place for the meat."

"The Apaches will know of this. Would it not be better to give it to them?"

"Ha! Señor Billy give meat to Apaches?"

"We will see." He went outside. The women were helping to butcher the dead animals. There were torches burning, and only Julio walked the perimeter of flickering light, watching the hills. Buchanan joined him.

Julio nodded at the blanketed form of the dead Apache. "The one called Moose. *Compadre* of Jo-san."

"It is a bitter night for Jo-san. Leaving his friend behind is a disgrace. The failure of the raid—more disgrace. You understand, Julio. But the young men do not understand."

Julio said, "The body should be returned. Meat should be given. The fighting should stop before many of us die."

"If you will pick out a pair of horses not so feisty as those I have seen," Buchanan suggested. "Steady pack animals, please. And your own mount, perhaps."

Julio looked to where Billy Button was overseeing the butchers. Then he smiled and vanished in the shadows.

Buchanan called, "Billy. A minute with you."

He came on his high-heeled boots, teetering a little, his face flushed. "I ain't goin' to give them damn Injuns a mouthful of nothin'," he declared.

"Feelin' ashamed like, are you?" Buchanan asked gently.

"I ain't no such of a damn . . ." Billy stopped. He could not meet Buchanan's eyes.

"Been sorta actin' up in town, haven't you? Neglectin' Nora, hangin' around with that fake Southern lady? Lost your big, bad bull because your boys are more onto fancy duds than steady work? Wouldn't listen to Julio or Salome or your old Uncle Tom?"

Billy said. "That ain't exactly the way it is. I mean, it ain't all that bad."

"No?"

"Well . . . Mando and the boys, they don't know about watchin' in the night. Not so good, anyway. I mean, they ain't fightin' men."

"You mean they haven't had experience and Mando and you didn't tell them to listen to Julio, who has experience," Buchanan said. "Now I am going to tell you somethin'. You had better get into town and watch over Nora and your baby."

"But what are you goin' to do?"

"I am going to take some of that red meat up to Juju. Apaches ain't like us, they don't bother about smoke houses and meat hangin' around. They like it the way it is now."

"I ain't goin' to do it!"

"Way I figured," said Buchanan cheerfully. "Therefore you better get to town right now. This minute. Then you won't be in my way when I do it."

"You're kowtowin' to a miserable little bunch of nothin'," Billy cried.

"Uh-huh. So long as I do the kowtowin', there's no skin off your elbow. So saddle up and get goin' before Jo-san raids into town. You got to remember that Coco is scared of guns and he can only whup so many Injuns at one time and Jo-san's got a half dozen, anyway."

"Town? You believe that sonbitch might . . .?"

Buchanan, who did not believe anything of the kind would happen this

126

particular night, said soberly, "You better get goin', Billy. I'm a tellin' you."

"Never thought of that. You right, Uncle Tom." He was going as fast as his tight boots would carry him. "Mando! Mando! Cut out my hoss! We goin' to town."

"Not Mando," Buchanan called after him. "Leave Mando here in charge of your boys."

Billy said, "Okay . . . okay, Uncle Tom."

Buchanan went to put a saddle on Nightshade. Julio had the pack animals waiting.

"You take Moose?" asked Julio.

"Yes. And have 'em load the other pack horse with meat."

"Señor Billy has not given the order."

Buchanan said, "Julio, I am a peaceable man. But maulin' a few little Mexican would-be cowboys wouldn't bother me one bit."

"I think Mando will listen," Julio said. "If not . . . I help you spank the small boys."

They watched Billy ride for town in all possible haste. They watched Mando turn back to the butchering. Then Julio spoke to the young foreman while Buchanan picked up the blanketed body of the dead Apache and slung him across the saddle of one of the pack animals, lashing him with care so that he would not slip.

Mando spread his hands, hunched his shoulders. He knew Buchanan—a glance was enough to keep him quiet. The other young *vaqueros* had nothing to say as they packed bloody meat into gunny sacks and arranged it across the broad back of the second pack horse.

Julio mounted. Buchanan led the way on Nightshade as they rode up into the hills under scudding clouds that threatened a storm. He still wore his six-gun and his rifle was ready in the boot. There was a chance that his errand of peace might turn out to be not so peaceful.

The night was empty of sound. Inside Buchanan's head there was only the feeling that although he was undertaking a gamble, it was a good bet—the odds were right. Julio, riding silent, seemed to agree. They rode with the unpleasant smell of the newly dead as they ascended the hill, deliberately without guile, wanting to be discovered by Juju's people.

The moon suddenly appeared amidst the clouds. They had reached the top of the hill, and they were skylined for several moments in the yellow-white glow. Julio made the bravado gesture of lighting a cigarette. They rode on, down a gentle slope, then upward through a box canyon, a steep path, slow going.

It was then that Buchanan knew they were there. He could actually feel Apaches again, as earlier. He spoke quietly to Nightshade, who was queasy around Indians. He did not have to say anything to Julio, whose ancestors had been fighting them for a thousand generations.

It was an older sentinel who came toward them. His hand was upraised. He called, questioning, "Buchanan?"

"Yes." They spoke in Spanish, a language natural to the Apache and to Buchanan.

"Juju said you would come."

"Juju is a chieftain."

The man grunted and turned, waving for them to follow. Inside a hundred yards they had to dismount and lead the horses through a narrow crevice, up a rocky road impossible to follow without a guide. They came to the encampment soon afterwards, a small flat surface in the rocks, where the Apaches could live like lizards for long periods of time.

A brave moved and a fire flared. Torches were lighted. Buchanan stood before them and spoke to Juju, who sat cross-legged at the fire with Emalita slightly behind him but almost touching him.

"I bring you the dead," Buchanan said.

"Yes. We see."

"And I bring you life—meat for your people."

"On the back of one pony," Juju said. "Beef that was killed by our own."

Buchanan looked around. "There are how many of you? A dozen? Can I feed a tribe? How much meat can I bring, a man with no cattle of his own?"

"Señor Button, he does not bring meat?"

"His prize bull is dead."

There was a rush of booted feet upon the rock and the slim figure of Jo-san appeared, flying at Buchanan's throat, a long knife in his hand. Julio reached and caught the shoulder of the youth, spinning him. Juju caught his wrist and disarmed him.

Jo-san crouched, spitting out the words. "The bull is dead! My brother, Juan Who Runs, lies there and you tell us the bull is dead!"

Buchanan said, "It was one way to get you out here where everybody can see you. Want to know why your brother is dead? Because you were fool enough to lead him to where men carry long guns and can shoot them."

"You killed him, Buchanan! The shot

131

came not from the stupidos of that ranch, but from where you stood."

"True," said Buchanan calmly. "And I would do it again to anyone who comes raiding."

"You will die, Buchanan! You will die slowly, with the splinters burning in you. You will die a hundred deaths, Buchanan!"

"That may well be," Buchanan told him. "But it won't be while I am not looking. Juju has said that your people are hungry. Feed them. I will try to bring more meat, later, when I have had time to make plans."

Jo-san's voice shrilled, "Beef is not the food to cleanse us of shame! Blood! Your blood, Buchanan, and that of your loud-mouth little friend Señor Button—and his wife and his son! Blood!"

Juju growled, "Enough! These men come in peace! Enough of your blather!"

Jo-san spread his arms. He was naked to the waist, he wore hair to his shoulders, the red headband, the high

132

leggins, traditional warrior garb. He called to the young men.

"Brothers. Will you come? Will you leave these old men? Will you join me in claiming our right, the blood of these white-eyes?"

There was no great acclamation, but he had scored, Buchanan knew. The young ones were moving apart. Emalita stood up, but they did not look to her, nor to Juju. They were totally with Jo-san. While the older men came closer to the fire and the chief, the youths moved out of the light of the flames.

Buchanan said, "I am sorry, Juju. You asked for meat, I give you meat to eat and be strong. I would try to fetch more, as I say. But if you cannot control the young braves, how can I do so?"

"I will counsel with my people," Juju said. It was as near as he dared come to saying that he would talk with Emalita.

Buchanan said, "We leave the pack animals. Use them, eat them if you must. You will hear from me again."

Juju said, "Go in peace."

The young men moved restlessly. Juju made a sign and the mature members of the band, those around the fire, produced weapons, which they turned upon Jo-san and his friends. No words were spoken but Buchanan felt relief as he mounted Nightshade and with the silent Julio by his side rode down out of the mountains.

4

BUCHANAN walked with Coco down Main Street in Encinal. People greeted them, many called, "Hey, good luck in the fight."

Coco waved but he also winced at each repetition of the good-natured salutation. Buchanan said nothing. It was mid-morning two days after the encounter out on the high plain.

Coco said, "I dunno just how it did happen, I keep tellin' you. There they was and there was Miss Nora and the baby and that gal Teresa and all. And there was money, bank money and all."

Buchanan said, "And there was that fast-talkin' Miss Heloise and her brother, if he is her brother, and the big fella, McMillan. It was some crowd, all right."

"Tom, you know I ain't scared of that big fella. You know I can handle him."

"Which is not the point. A con game

135

don't depend on anything as chancy as a fight. Not unless they got some way of puttin' you out of business."

"You wouldn't let 'em do that."

"Right. But you know they got another way to fix things. Remember? They get people to bet on their man, they get somebody to cover with their money? Then he lays down to you and they collect and run."

"But you wouldn't let 'em pull that one, neither," said Coco triumphantly.

"It's just that we don't know what they are plannin'," Buchanan said. "Let me talk to this banker fella. He's new since I was here."

Hamilton Mizer seemed to be waiting for them. He had two other gentlemen, Mr. Chatterton—a lawyer—and Marshal Beaumont. Both were smiling. The banker never smiled.

Buchanan greeted them, sat down in a chair, and crossed his legs. Coco sat beside him. They waited.

Mizer said, "Ahem. Uh—the boxing match, isn't it?"

"I'm not here to deposit money in your

lousy bank," Buchanan told him. "Although if all is squared away I might put up a few dollars."

"Put up money? For the purse?"

"Not likely! That's your problem. I know it hurts, but you agreed. Coco put up his share. Na—I'm for betting that Coco will win."

"How much, suh?" asked Beaumont.

Ignoring him, Buchanan asked the banker, "How much is your mortgage on that hotel across the street?"

"Well . . . uh . . . I don't see—"

Buchanan interrupted. "I'll bet the amount of that mortgage, either on the paper the bank holds or against cash which I see in the hands of a stakeholder. I'll bet it all that Coco knocks out this great fighter of yours."

"Knocks him out? You're jokin', suh," said Beaumont.

"I don't joke about Coco's ability," Buchanan said.

Beaumont said eagerly to the banker and the lawyer, "McMillan has never ever been knocked down! Surely you all will want to accept this challenge, gentlemen!"

Mizer said, "I never bet. Never will."

"I don't care where the money comes from," Buchanan said. "Get it up—or there may not be a fight."

Lawyer Chatterton said, "Just a minute now. The fight has been agreed upon."

"Has it?"

Chatterton, Mizer, and Beaumont exchanged stares.

Buchanan said, "You got a signature on a piece of paper?"

"Bean has put up two thousand dollars. It would be forfeited if he ran out on the bout," said Chatterton. "I can assure you of that."

Buchanan leaned back and smiled. "Gentlemen, if we wanted to run out, we would take that money back and go our way. We don't want to. But since Coco was hustled into accepting by a con job and since you people are so anxious, I intend to make a profit. So . . . get up the money. I'd kinda like to own that hotel, such a nice, new buildin' and all. I could fire some more of the help, get the town a new marshal, and maybe stick around a while. Have some fun."

"How dare you, suh!" Beaumont cried. "I and my sister and others, we want this bout to be advertised, to bring people to Encinal, to make us famous here. You are not a citizen of this town, suh."

"Mister," said Buchanan, "I was here when this town was a crossroad. And a better place than it is now. But that ain't it: I want to know where the fight takes place, the exact day and time of day. I want to know who is going to referee. And I want to be damn sure everything is on the level."

"The town's honor is at stake," said Chatterton. He was a portly man with a florid complexion. "You may certainly depend upon us."

"I expect to." He got up. He looked at them for a long moment. "I sure do. So get busy, gentlemen. And you, also, Beaumont."

He nodded and walked out, Coco at his side. They went down the street to the general store, and Buchanan bought a canvas sack and some rope. They carried it up to the carriage house, and Coco filled the sack with red sand while Buchanan set up a rigging for it. Coco now had a heavy punching bag. There was enough left to make a skipping rope.

Buchanan said, "Two weeks. It's not enough to get you in top shape. So we plan for a quick knockout."

"I ain't never outa shape," Coco protested.

"And keep one eye on the house all the time," Buchanan ordered. He was still upset by the situation in which they found themselves, at the attitudes of the banker and the lawyer and the smugness of Elton Beaumont. "I'm going to see what I can dig up about this McMillan. And maybe find somebody to spar with you."

Coco said slyly, "Why, Tom, I got you to train me. Don't need nobody else."

"Uh-huh." This was an ancient ploy. Since their first meeting in an El Paso jail, when Buchanan had thrown Coco through a boarded-up window to freedom, the hunt had been on. Coco never did believe that Buchanan was the better man. A hundred times he had tried to get a match going, bare-fist or with gloves. And a hundred times Buchanan had either been newly wounded or simply disinclined to hurt—or be hurt by—a friend.

Coco was donning his tights and jersey. He carried his gear in a carpetbag worn from much travel. He had bandages to protect his knuckles, gloves for striking the bag, pillow-gloves for sparring. He had soft leather shoes and ankle braces.

Buchanan watched him. He was very fond of his friend, and he knew there was a trick in this match, something more than met the eye. He would have to ferret it out. Disgustedly, he swung a fist at the dangling sandbag.

The heavy bag swung to the extent of the rope on which it hung, came hurtling back. At the end of the arc the rope broke. Coco, donning ready-made training bandages, stopped and stared.

"Okay, let's get it back up again," Buchanan said. The action had released a lot of tension. He patiently repaired the damage, restrung the bag, and hung it from a rafter.

Coco said from a contemplative silence. "But I dunno if you could land that one on me."

"You never will know." Buchanan grinned at him. "Leastways not if I can help it."

Coco danced around on the hard dirt floor. He jabbed and hooked at the air, shadowboxing. Teresa came from the house, curious, carrying Thomas Mulligan. Nora, in her sunbonnet and overalls, wandered around the edge of the barn and joined them. Coco rolled his eyes and showed his gold tooth and kept on with his long-established routine: the shadowboxing, the heavy bag, the exercises. He would start running tomorrow, although Buchanan had warned him not to head for the hills where the Apache youths were certainly skulking. The women and the baby watched with wide eyes.

Buchanan went to the stable. He was

saddling up Nightshade when Billy appeared, dressed for the town.

Billy said, "I'll ride in with you, okay?"

"Better you should stay here and keep a gun handy," Buchanan told him. "Coco will back you up—but like I keep telling you, not with a gun. If Jo-san—or anyone else—comes down from the hills you'll need guns."

Billy asked, "Have I got to stay around the house all the time?"

"You better had." Buchanan was short with him. "You act like you got the itch or something. Take care of your family, Billy. That's your job for now."

He rode Nightshade out of the yard and into Encinal. He was not pleased with Billy Button. He wanted to know a lot more about Big Jim McMillan and whatever he could learn about Heloise and Elton Beaumont. He wanted to find out how far from town Dolan and Griff had traveled. And all the while he worried about Jo-san and the young Apaches.

Jo-san was hungry. Sometimes his mind

143

wavered, he saw bright flashes, like lightning. He had refused to eat the meat brought by Buchanan. He had led his five remaining young men to a camp apart from Juju and Emalita and the others. He had made his brag that he would bring down Billy Button and Buchanan.

The other young braves had eaten. They were lounging in the sunshine near a cold mountain stream that wandered down into the lower hills overlooking Encinal. From this vantage point much of the town's activities could be spied upon and a scouting expedition after dark could be easily accomplished. But he needed strength.

He had set a trap downstream. There was almost no game in the hills, but he had to try. It was difficult being a leader —and he a halfbreed—and he had to make every little deed count. When he heard the snap and whirr of the string as it drew taut he made himself walk slowly and with dignity to where a jackrabbit, scrawny enough at that, dangled helplessly.

He dispatched the creature with the knife he had retrieved from Juju. Thought of his father's displeasure and his mother's sad disapproval made him even more uncomfortable as he kindled the fire he had set in bold preparation for his meal.

The others looked on with some awe, now. They spoke among themselves, nodding, not interrupting Jo-san as he skinned, gutted, and spitted the rabbit. None of them had been able to catch as much as a land turtle or a crow. They all felt guilty for having eaten the red meat while Jo-san refrained.

It was not enough, however. He had to accomplish more, Jo-san felt. The musket lay alongside him; he now despised it. Once it had been a prize. Since he had missed Buchanan, since Moose had been killed, he knew the musket was no good to him. He had to have another weapon besides his well-honed knife.

He still smarted at the way he had been disarmed in the camp. In another moment he would have cut Buchanan's throat.

He brooded over the broiling rabbit, hungering more for Buchanan's blood than for the tough, stringy meat he knew would be forthcoming.

He had good teeth. He chewed the rabbit down to the bone and sucked out the marrow. He wiped his knife on a clump of furze and went to the stream and washed his hands of the grease and drank from them, cooling his face by dipping it into the cool water.

Now he turned his attention to his silent companions. "You see, my medicine, it worked."

They all nodded eager agreement.

"So I will also trap the white-eye, Buchanan." He paused, then said, "It was a mistake to attack the ranchero. There are too many guns in that place. Until we have guns of our own, we must attack the town."

The others moved uneasily, and a brave called Lone Piñon asked, "Are there not more guns in the town?"

"Yes, but not the men to shoot straight. You saw the man who led, the

146

ones who followed. He who wears the star is a fool, the others are worse. If we go in at night we will find guns and bullets. Then we will steal the baby of Billy Button."

"The baby?"

Jo-san fixed Lone Piñon with a steely gaze. "You don't know the weakness of such as Buchanan? The woman and the baby—he would give up his life to save them. And we will accept the exchange. We will take his life and that of Billy Button, that other fool."

"And the woman and baby?"

"We will give them to Juju and to Emalita for slaves!" This seemed his best idea yet; he was fond of the notion of forgiving his mother and father and of presenting them gifts to prove his generosity. He forgot that Emalita had conceived the idea of the kidnapping.

The five young men thought about this. The boldness of it appealed to them. They finally nodded unanimous agreement to the plan.

Jo-san said, "I will now scout alone. I will go to the town and learn what I can. You remain here, out of sight and out of harm's way."

He strode off down the hill, hoping that he left them with the feeling that they could not act without his orders. The loss of Moose had depleted his stature, he knew. He found that he was lonely without his big friend. He went faster, boldly, toward Encinal with the lust for vengeance running hot through his body and soul.

He chose a familiar path, leading down past long-played-out and consequently deserted mine shafts. There was almost no chance of meeting anyone in this area, he thought. He had the knack of keeping out of sight; he was slight, and he could take on the coloration of his surroundings like a native lizard.

He was making his way within two miles of town when he heard a muffled explosion. He stopped in his tracks, sought a round, red rock and melted into it, motionless, straining his ears. He was almost at the mouth of a mine shaft that had once spewed out ore for the stamp mill at Encinal. He knew enough about such matters; he had, as Buchanan surmised, been at mission school long enough to learn Yanqui ways and Yanqui speech.

He began to stir, thinking to move closer and eavesdrop. If there was gold in this abandoned mine he wanted to know about it. There would be nothing to steal since the ore was useless until it had been through the mill, but men who dug for precious stuff had guns and ammunition and dynamite and this could be stolen with great gain.

Before he could leave the shelter of the red rock he heard the tinkle of harness and the clop-clop of hooves and the slight squeak of a carriage wheel. He fell back and waited.

The man with the star, dressed in gray, was driving the buggy. Beside him was the woman from the hotel whom he called his sister. They tied up the horse and got down from the buggy and went into the mouth of the cave, the woman walking delicately, like all white squaws. Jo-san crept out from the rock, then, and followed, knowing there was not the slightest chance that these two people would discover him. He doubted they would see him even if they turned around and stared. They were not of the Western land, therefore they were blind.

When he had got part way into the shaft, which descended abruptly, he lay down and listened. He could listen almost as well as a full-blooded Apache because he had worked at it, imitating their terrific powers of concentration. He made out the voices, then began to distinguish the words.

The woman said, "How are you doing, Freddy?"

"Good enough," said the man named Freddy.

"Mac, what do you think?"

"I think he's doin' fine. I think I better get the hell outa here and start real trainin' for the nigger."

"You'll beat the nigger," said the man

with the badge. "I am bettin' everything on you."

The woman said, "You haven't got anything, Elton. *We* are betting. And Mac is right. He should be where people can see him, know he is training. There'll be strangers in town. The bank has sent out dodgers all over Arizona and Texas. Chatterton got a special dispensation from the governor to hold the fight. Since this is still a territory he was able to get support all the way to Albuquerque."

All this did not make any sense to Jo-san. He would have to go to town and hear some more. Then he could sit down and think it through and put it all together. Meantime, what of the gold?

The big man said, "We've blowed this shaft apart. Too bad there wasn't any pay dirt left. Anyways, Freddy won't have any trouble blowin' up that tin safe in Mizer's bank."

"That's all we want to know," the woman said. Like Emalita she seemed to be the leader. Jo-san scowled. It was the same the world over, it seemed: let a woman have a word to say and she took over the tribe.

But now they were coming out of the shaft, the badge man and the woman and the big man. Jo-san recognized the giant; he was one who stood out in Encinal, a friend of the lady and Freddy and the badge man. The woman and the marshal got into the buggy.

The big man said, "You niggle along there. I'll run with you. It's only a couple miles. I need to do a lot of runnin' for the legs."

"They don't know how quick you are," said the woman admiringly. "They're going to get the shock of their life. You keep him moving, make it exciting, that'll do it. We'll take care of everything else. With the betting and all, there should be thousands extra in that bank."

"I'm countin' on it," said the big fellow. "And if you people should get any ideas of runnin' out on me . . . I got plenty time and plenty reason to chase you down and scrag you, both of you, nice and slow until you bust."

"Don't talk silly," said the woman. "Have I ever let you down?"

"It's never been worth your while," said the fighter.

"It never will be," she assured him.

Jo-san, behind his rock, knew she was lying. It was amazing how white-eyes did not recognize plain, flat liars when they heard one. The very honey in her voice proclaimed that the woman was not telling the truth.

He let them get out of sight. Then he took a secondary route to town. He had plenty of time, dusk was the best for him; he could move after sundown without being discovered. He went over the conversation he had heard. He did not understand much of it. His mission training had not been that extensive—truthfully he had been a bad student. But he did believe he had discovered one fact: Those people were going to blow up the bank in Encinal.

The big man running behind the horse and carriage, that was another matter. Talk of a "fight" meant only a battle with

153

guns and knives and bows and arrows, but evidently those people had another meaning. He wondered if it had anything to do with Buchanan.

He was obsessed by Buchanan's presence in the country. He had been humiliated, disgraced by the big man, not once but twice. Whatever he did, whatever he schemed, Buchanan had to suffer. And while he was at it that big-mouth, stingy, lucky little Billy Button would suffer also, he vowed.

After all, Buchanan and he were as one. He walked slowly, his knife hand in his belt, but there was no sign of a living creature that would be edible. He made a long circle to the north. He knew why he was going this way, but he denied it to himself for an hour. It was still daylight when he had reached the back of the house in which the Averys dwelt. He sank down behind a convenient clump of buffalo grass and wrestled with himself.

His stomach was so empty it thought his throat was cut, he imagined. He had sworn never to take a handout from a white-eye again so long as he drew breath. But the truth was, he might not be able to draw breath if he did not eat soon. The skinny rabbit had not stayed with him, his strength was ebbing fast. He came out from behind the brush and shoved the knife down deep in his leggin so that Miz Avery would not detect it. He sauntered into the backyard, threading his way past nasturtiums and geraniums and other blossoms much prized by the lady, he remembered. He hesitated at the door.

He need not have worried. Miz Avery flung the door open, put her hands on her hips, and said severely, "Joe! I saw you wanderin' around out there. You come in this kitchen immediately, you hear me?"

He said, "Yes'm." She liked that. Before she had sent him to the mission she had taught him a few things that pleased her. Politeness was one of them.

She said, "I do declare, you're as skinny as an eel. Not that you'd know what an eel looks like, which is just as well . . . You set right down there at that table. I got a leftover dish of hash'll heat up in a minute. And there's soup on the stove, like always. You want to he'p yourself to the soup? You do that and don't spill none on my clean kitchen floor, neither."

"No, ma'am," he said. He knew about the soup, always on, added to at every meal, all the good tidbits, all the rich, fine meats and vegetables. "I'd just as soon have the soup and never mind the hash. Thank you, ma'am."

She was already bustling with a frying pan, putting the hash on, stirring up the fire. "You'll eat what I tell you. You always did. And you can tell me where you been and what you been doin' since you ran away from the mission."

He slurped soup and managed to say, "They wasn't good to me like you, Miz Avery." He hated himself for aping the speech of these people, but it was in a good cause. He kept reminding himself: It would keep him alive and strong.

"You was always wild. You never accepted the Lord. But one thing I'll say for you," Miz Avery told him. "You didn't pretend. A lot of them Indians made believe they were converted."

"Yes'm," he said. The soup was thicker than usual, and it tasted better than anything he had eaten since the last time he was here in Encinal. He never had been a full Apache where food was concerned . . . but then, he wasn't a full-blooded Indian; he was half Mexican.

She said, still fussing over the hash, "This town is just as bad. They got a big prizefight arranged now. That's agin the Lord and all the teachin's of Jesus. But they want a show, they want to wager. Even that nice Mr. Buchanan is into this with his black fighter. And Heloise Beaumont who is no better than she should be, if you ask me. Which you didn't of course."

"No'm." He had finished the soup. Now the thought of the hash was pleasant. "Mr. Avery all right these days?"

"Fine, just fine. Only he thinks the prizefight is a good idea, good for the town. That McMillan, he's a bad un, and the marshal's in on it and all. People ain't even thinkin' about the christenin' of Billy Button's baby."

"No'm?" He knew about christening. That's what he wouldn't stay for at the mission. So they were going to do it to the baby of the rotten, rich Button. Maybe that would be a good time to come in and . . . No, that was wrong. There would be too many of them around.

She said, "Half the town'll be at the church. Instead of havin' their minds on holy things, they'll be talkin' about the prizefight, and who'll win. I know 'em!"

The hash was now steaming. He sat and looked at it. His mouth watered. The soup had been wonderful and the hash would just put a finish on it. She took bread out of the oven, unwrapping it, then slicing it with a huge knife. There was butter from the cooling box and jam too, homemade blackberry jam. He wiped the moisture from the corners of his mouth. It was almost worth being so hungry to sit there and know that he was going to be so well fed.

He ate and even when he was finished it didn't seem to him that he was entirely full. He thanked Miz Avery again.

She said, "Up to some devilment, I suppose. Your mama, Emalita, is a fine lady. Your papa is out causin' trouble, they tell me. Now, here is bread and butter and some of the cold meat I just happen to have. See, I'm wrappin' it good for you. Now, you take this and remember that if you follow the teachin's of Jesus and walk in the footsteps of the Lord, you will live happy and come to a righteous end." She stared at him, then shook her head. "You'll never do it. Well, anyway, you won't starve for a little while."

He said, "No'm. Thank you again, Miz Avery."

He was going out of the yard, carrying the food as if it were more precious than gold, when he thought of something. He turned back along the side of the house. Miz Avery was in the kitchen, singing a hymn, cleaning up. He came to an open window. He put down the bundle of food

159

and slid over the sill. He rummaged around for a minute, careful to restore every item to its proper place.

It was in the middle drawer. He lifted it out and stuck it in his waistband. He got out of the house, picked up the food, and headed for the middle of town.

It was a good thing he had thought of the revolver that Avery kept but never used. It was loaded, too. He might be able to steal some ammunition for it now that twilight was coming on. The purple shadows encouraged him. They were very beautiful, and they gave him cover.

Now he had to think about the prize-fight. The big man was in it, and Miz Avery had mentioned Buchanan and a black man. Jo-san had seen a few black men before Beaumont had chased them all out of Encinal. But he had not seen Buchanan's black man.

He made a detour around the town. He felt strong now. He came up behind the Button house on the hill. There were lights in the house and a lantern shone in the carriage house.

Jo-san found a flat rock and made a cache of his food and sat for a moment. He felt loaded down with the revolver, so he put that with the package from Miz Avery. He was not going to waste precious ammunition tonight. Even if he got Buchanan in the sights he would not shoot. That could wait, now. He wanted to know more about the prizefight, about the black man. After a few moments he sneaked down behind the carriage house and applied his eye to a crack in the boards.

A lantern was hung high. A heavy, peculiar bag was strung from the rafters. Buchanan stood behind the bag, holding onto it.

A muscular man was slugging the bag with his fists. He was black, all right. Buchanan spoke to him. "Faster! You got to make it fast this time!"

The black man grunted, and his fists moved with bewildering speed, slamming the bag. Buchanan gave a little under the pounding, and this seemed to please him, for he cried, "That's the way to go! That's better!"

The black man rested. Sweat gleamed on him. He said, "We got lots of time. I'll be ready for this fight."

"I believe you," Buchanan said. "But this McMillan is a very big man. He may be very tough."

"I seen 'em as tough as they git," the black man said, doubling up the huge fists. "It don't make no never mind how tough they are."

Buchanan said, "It's a prizefight. You got a referee, which will be a local man who might have a bet on McMillan. And there's somethin' else goin' on, I keep tellin' you. I want you to make it quicker than quick."

"If you'd just put the big mittens on with me," the black man said, "it sure would help a lot."

Buchanan said, "I don't have time for that. I got other things to do."

The black man said, "That ain't what's holdin' you back and you know it."

"Okay. You're right," Buchanan said. "It's just that I wouldn't want to risk hurtin' you with the fight less 'n two weeks away."

With that he went out the door. The black man looked after him and shook his head. Then he grinned and went back to hitting the bag, not so hard this time, dancing and prancing in a peculiar, rhythmic, shuffling fashion, almost like an Indian dance. Jo-san would have liked to go in and talk with the black man and find out all about the fight for a prize and how Buchanan was connected with it and the exact time it was going to take place. But he could see that the black and Buchanan were good friends beneath their yelling at one another.

He decided he had better steal some ammunition for Mr. Avery's gun and retrieve the food and get back to his five remaining followers. He would also loot the store for some more food if he got the chance. He wished he could steal a horse. He even debated trying for one of Billy Button's horses, but there was Buchanan and also the strong, heavyweight black man. He maneuvered toward the store where the guns and bullets were kept.

5

BUCHANAN watched while Marshal Beaumont checked the rear window of Jake Stein's general store, fussed around with the list of missing supplies, then nodded firmly and departed. Mr. Avery stood by.

Buchanan said, "Reckon he does his investigatin' in the bar of the hotel."

"That's right," said Avery.

Jake Stein said, "Remember when Billy stole them things from me? He left the money—part of it, anyway. Paid it in full when he sold the Bucket o' Blood."

"Want me to look around?" Buchanan asked. "Un-official, like?"

"Wish you would," said Jake Stein. "I got an idea but I'd like to check it with you."

Buchanan went outdoors and around to the back window of the store. It had been pried open. There were marks on the sill, but there were no footprints below the window. Avery came and peered at the ground, then shook his head.

"No use lookin' further. I got to tell you somethin'. Private, of course."

Buchanan had moved twenty feet away from the window. He got down on one knee, put his nose close to earth. Then he arose and said, "One small, skinny Indian."

"Yeah," said Avery. "I know."

"How do you know, Ed?"

"On account of Miz Avery, consarn her and her charity."

"She fed him. Jo-san. She calls him 'Joe' on account of she knew him since he was a button. Sent him to the mission school, a lot of good that did."

"Well, he was hungry, all right. Prob'ly too proud to eat the meat we took to them."

"Sure. Feedin' him is all right. But the little bastard stole my gun."

Buchanan sobered. "Now, that is bad. He had a smooth-bore old musket. Couldn't hit a barn door in moonlight."

"Mine's a .45 Colt double action," said Avery miserably. "And Jake says he missed some ammunition for it. That there is the second window Jo-san skinned through yesterday. First he got my pistol. Then he got the food and the bullets."

Buchanan was thoughtful. "If he was around town he must have been out to Billy's house. I wonder if he thought up any mischief out there?"

"He was always a maverick. Maybe because of his mixed blood. Maybe he was born mean. Miz Avery, she always claims he's real nice to her. He's smart enough to play that game."

"His mother has plenty brains," Buchanan said. "His father's got good sense. The crooked damn Indian agent gives 'em plenty reason for going out. The biggest reason, hunger."

Avery sighed. "I know. I've written Washington more 'n once. Might's well save the postage."

"Government won't do anything.

Never did, never will. People ought to learn that even Apaches are folks."

"Jo-san is folks, all right. Bad folks!"

"He's a rascal, true enough." Buchanan went back to the front of the store. Avery followed closely. "You won't spread it around? About my wife?"

"Course not, Ed. Anyway, I ain't the law. Marshal Beaumont is the law all by himself, with Dolan chased out of town."

"He deputized Freddy Daggett this mornin'," Jake Stein informed them. "They make a fine pair."

"Of deuces," said Avery. "After the prizefight this town had better get wise to itself."

"Can't do nothin' until the fight's over," Stein agreed. He looked at Buchanan. "Folks'll be comin' in next week. Your man gettin' ready?"

"He'll be ready."

Stein said, "Well, I lost a few dollars in food and one thing and another. I'll try to get it back bettin' on Coco Bean."

"He'll give you his best."

Avery said, "I ain't a betting man. And

if Miz Avery ever caught me . . . but I'm puttin' a hundred up at the bank. Did you hear where Mizer's actin' as stakeholder?"

Buchanan said, "I'm on my way there now."

He left the assayer and the merchant and went along the street to the bank. Hamilton Mizer was behind his desk as usual. Buchanan entered and loomed over him.

Mizer asked, "What can I do for you, Mr. Buchanan?"

"That mortgage. You want to bet it against cash?"

Mizer said, "It's a lot of money for a small-town banker to wager."

"How much?"

"Five thousand." The prune face narrowed. "Cash."

Buchanan unbuckled the money belt from around his waist. He counted out five thousand dollars in crisp, new paper money, green bills with gold backs.

"The bank can't make a bet," said Mizer. "You know that."

"The banker can. You know *that*."

Mizer could not remove his eyes from the fresh, tantalizing money. "I suppose that's different."

"Don't forget, I'm bettin' Coco knocks him out."

"Taken!" said Mizer. He picked up the money and counted it reverently. "Knocks him out. Right!"

Buchanan asked, "Now tell me, where is the fight to he held?"

"On the west side of town," Mizer said. "The bank—er—holds some property. It is mostly flat land, somewhat sandy. Fine for growing vegetables. We will erect the ring upon it."

"Who's goin' to sell lots?" Buchanan asked. "Or are you just goin' to plaster it with for-sale signs?"

"If anyone wishes to purchase, we will have people to take their—er—orders."

"Their cash, you mean? After they win bettin' on McMillan to stay?"

"You could look at it that way. Business is business."

"Every day and every minute. I'm sure

glad I ain't in it. Business, I mean," said Buchanan. "Takes so doggone much of a man's time. You want to give me a receipt for that five thousand?"

"Why, of course. Certainly."

But he would not have done so, Buchanan thought, had he not been asked. He was typical of the people who were coming into the territory, of the loud-voiced, hugely praised band who were to "bring civilization to the West."

Buchanan put away the receipt and said, "On a Sunday, did they tell me? Miz Avery won't like that."

"We moved it back to Saturday," Mizer said. "At four in the afternoon, when the sun is not so strong. Everything in town will be closed down. It is a big event and will bring much business to Encinal."

"Good for you," said Buchanan. "Then you won't miss the mortgage interest and all when you lose the hotel and gimme back my five thousand."

He left before Mizer could do more

than choke on the very thought of losing. Still feeling rather ornery, he crossed the street and went into the hotel. There was a stranger at the desk. Freddy Daggett was behind the bar, and Heloise sat on the high lookout stool. There were no poker players and very few customers. Beaumont was laying out solitaire on the green baize top of a table.

Buchanan said, "Whiskey, please."

"Yes, sir," said Daggett. He raised an eyebrow and made a small ceremony of putting forth bottle and glass. "Anything else, sir?"

"Not right now," said Buchanan. "I see the marshal is runnin' down clues on the robbery."

Daggett said maliciously, "Yes, sir. That's his way of cogitating."

Heloise giggled. Beaumont looked up and for an instant Buchanan saw the inner fire, the intensity, the violence concealed beneath the exterior of foppish clothes. It was the manner of the bigoted Southerner. The man, he realized in surprise, was truly dangerous. He had been wrong about this mob being strictly on the con. They were all capable of much more than the gentle grift.

Heloise came down from her perch with her customary display of silken ankle and moved between Beaumont and the bar. She said, clapping her hands together, "Mr. Buchanan will have his little joke, I do declare!"

Beaumont said, "Yes . . . a jest . . . of course."

Buchanan widened his eyes. "Nope. I often get my thinkin' done over a game of solitaire. Nothin' strange about it. Thought I might tell you, though. It was a skinny little Indian, plenty hungry. Jake ain't makin' any charges."

Beaumont said, "Juju, no doubt?"

"Nope. Smaller and lighter on his feet."

"And pray tell me, how do you know that?" demanded the marshal.

"Track. I looked around and there was track. Livin' in the wilds, a man learns those things."

"Track? Oh . . . footprints? But how

173

could you possibly decide footprints discovered today are those of a thief who worked his deed last night?" demanded Beaumont.

Buchanan heaved a deep breath. "Now, that would require a heap of talk. Like the way the tracks look if there's been a heavy dew or if there hasn't and a lot of things like that. It's not very interesting."

Beaumont said. "In other words, you can't be absolutely certain, is that it?"

"Oh, I'm certain enough. Thing is, you're the law, I'm just a citizen. It's you that has the responsibility."

"I fail to see responsibility on my part if Stein isn't goin' to prefer cha'ges, suh."

Buchanan said, "Okay, if that's the way you see it."

"And how else, pray?"

"Well, if one skinny Indian boy can break in and steal food and ammunition, what if a whole gang came in some night? And used the bullets to shoot anybody who tried to keep 'em from food?"

"This town would know how to defend itself," Beaumont declared. "This town is ready for anything that Apache dog has in his quiver, believe me, suh!"

"I see." Buchanan finished his drink. "Glad you got everybody alerted."

Heloise held out her arms. "Lift me onto the bar, please, and I'll buy a drink, Mr. B. I'm too little to stand up there with real men."

He caught her under the arms and swung her high and sat her down. She clapped her hands in delight and cried, "I declare, Mr. B, you *are* the strongest man. I don't b'lieve McMillan is as strong as you!"

Daggett pushed the bottle to Buchanan and brought out another glass and a pitcher of water, grinning. "McMillan wouldn't like to hear that. He reckons he's the biggest and best these days. Training always makes him sore as a bear."

"Shame on him, then," she said. She mixed whiskey and water and raised her glass. "Here's to the big fight."

Buchanan nodded, drinking. "Hope it's

a success for the hotel. And I do hope I win the mortgage."

"You wouldn't foreclose on us, now, would you, Mr. B?" She batted her eyes.

He said, "Not so long as you paid the interest. Might buy you out, though if Coco wins."

"Buy me out?" She stared at him with a calculating little smile on her lips. "Why Mr. B, I don't believe I want to sell. And you're not goin' to win your bet."

"We'll see in good time." Buchanan looked at Daggett. "You heard anything about who the town selected to referee?"

"I did." He nodded toward Beaumont. "They had a meeting and elected the marshal, there."

"Well, now." It was just as well to have him up there in plain view at that, Buchanan thought. He cocked his head to one side and asked. "You had some experience handlin' bare-knuckle fights, marshal?"

"I have, suh. In the South we fought our niggers quite often."

"I see." He sipped the drink, stifling

his anger. He knew about "fightin' our niggers." He knew the agony, win or lose, suffered by the helpless black men. "Well, this is a bit different, you know. I'll be in Coco's corner."

"I do wish I could see it," Heloise cried. "Why do they keep women from seein' prizefights?"

"They are not for the eyes of a lady," Beaumont said. "They are brutal exhibitions."

Buchanan said, "It'll be right lonely here in town for you, Miss Beaumont. Seems like everyone's goin' to be out there on the flats that day."

She said, "Mr. Mizer's flat land. Ho! You know about that?"

"I heard."

"They'll be out there. And he'll take them if he can, the old skinflint."

Daggett said, "That's one reason I'm glad I'm on duty that day."

"Are you goin' to miss the bout?" Buchanan perked up his ears. Daggett, he thought, would not stay away without a good reason.

"Have to keep Heloise company. Truth is, I never was much for fights," Daggett said.

"Uh-huh. I've known a lot of people that way," Buchanan said. "Don't like to see men get hurt."

"Oh, I don't mind," Daggett said. "If they killed each other, now, as in ancient Rome. If they were gladiators, then I would enjoy it."

Heloise said, "Freddy, you are bad! You are a really bad man!"

"He's also lyin'," Beaumont said. He finished his game, slid the cards together with less than expert hands. He came to the bar and said, "You need not worry about me being the referee, Buchanan. McMillan is a fine boxer. I know his style. I will accommodate both men as they deserve."

"You do that," Buchanan told him. "Glad to know it's been settled. I'd better go on up to Billy's, now."

"We haven't seen Billy," Heloise said, pouting. "Why's he keepin' to himself these evenin's?"

"There was a threat against his family," Buchanan told her. "There was also a fight out at the graze. We figure Juju's too smart to attack if anyone is around and looking for him."

"So Billy's guardin' the home fires?" Beaumont laughed. "That should be nice for him."

"I don't hear any complaints." He nodded to them and left the hotel and walked toward the Button place. He had to pass the little house that Grampaw Mulligan had built for Nora. It was locked up, but it had been maintained in good order, even to the weeding of the garden, he saw. Nora could never forget that little place.

And Billy was getting restless. He believed Billy would have returned to the hotel bar despite the fact that he knew Heloise and the others were crooks. The old story: "It's the only game in town." True, there was no other night life in Encinal, excepting the cantina where the Mexicans drank tequila or beer.

Maybe he should send Billy into town.

It was worth thinking about. Maybe Billy could learn something about the scheme that Heloise and company had ready for the day of the big fight. Because there *was* a plan; Buchanan was as sure of it as he was sure that they were dishonest. If he could even guess at the plan he would know what to do.

With Beaumont in the ring, the game had to be played by Daggett, the two missing members, Dolan and Griff, and Heloise. The question was, what could they do? The safe in the bank was as big as a small room and strongly built. Mizer kept all the cash in that vault.

There must be something, Buchanan thought, walking up the hill toward the new house that Billy had built. Nora was sitting on the top step of the veranda.

She was wearing her garden costume of overalls, a man's shirt, and tiny boots made by hand in El Paso. She was grimy from her work, her pretty face smudged. He came up to her, took off his neckerchief, and dabbed at her.

"Girl as good lookin' as you shouldn't

set around like a dirty-face kid," he told her.

Tears started, making his task easier. He sat down beside her, and she put her head on his shoulder. He let her nestle there for a few moments. He could hear Coco working out in the carriage house, Teresa in the kitchen singing a Mexican song to Thomas Mulligan Button. There was neither sight nor sound of the master of the house.

"Where's Billy?" he asked.

The tears stopped. Nora's head came up, defiant. "I don't know and I don't care."

"Goodness me," said Buchanan. "I thought yawl got over fightin' and scratchin' back in the old days."

"We did," she said. "Now we don't talk at all."

"I wouldn't call that an improvement."

"I wouldn't neither," she said. "Oh, Uncle Tom, I wish we were back in my own little house."

"It's still there, all right. But it looks a sight more comfortable up here."

"You know, when we ran away to El Paso and got married I thought I was in heaven. We had money from Grandpaw's mine, we seemed to have everything. Billy had cash from selling the Bucket o' Blood, too. We bought what we wanted and enjoyed everything so much!"

"That was just fine. Course it couldn't last forever, now, could it?"

"No. That's what I'm finding out. Less 'n two years ago Billy couldn't do enough for me. Even when we built this house, all the while living in the old one, it was exciting, an adventure. He was wonderful."

"Then you got in the family way."

She said, "That made Billy all the happier. He kept talking about a boy, how he wanted a son, how he had no family that he knew of and this would make us a family. Oh, we talked about that a lot."

"Well, seems like Thomas Mulligan is a boy, all right."

"An ugly little boy baby." She giggled through the tears that lingered in her eyes. "Boys can be ugly, that's all right. I bet Billy was ugly as a mud fence when he was a baby."

"Could be." Billy was still no beauty, Buchanan thought but did not say. "Anyway . . . what's the trouble now, darlin'?"

She said, "Billy. He just don't pay any attention to me. I hate the way I live. I hate it!"

"The way you live seems all right to me," said Buchanan, honestly bewildered. "This is a nice place, you got the baby and your garden and anything you need, haven't you?"

"I've got Teresa to take care of the baby. There's a woman comes in and does the heavy work once a week. I don't have to get up in the morning unless I want to. And yes, I've got my garden."

"Sounds good to me."

She said, "It's awful!"

He thought of his mother back in East Texas and how she had arisen at daybreak —sometimes earlier—to get breakfast for husband, son, and hired help. And how she had done the chores while the sheriff-father did his job and the son worked the cotton field with the black people. It had been sultry in that part of the country, and she was always hot, perspiring. And when her husband was killed she had just up and died, worn out and unable to face the world with a teen-age son to care for.

He said, "Reckon I can guess the trouble."

"I wish I was back with Grampaw!"

"Without the baby?"

"*With* the baby!"

Buchanan said slowly. "What you really want, darlin', is to be right where you are, to have the baby and Teresa—and to have some excitement."

"Anything but this dumb life!"

"Uh-huh. And that's what Billy wants."

"Billy? He's got the hotel saloon. And . . . that . . . that woman."

"Had to get to that sooner or later," he told her. "That woman got caught cheatin' the other night, you know."

"It's not just her. Any kind of fun and

excitement is what he craves. His . . . his wife and son ain't enough for him anymore." The tears flowed again.

Buchanan said, "Nora, seems to me like you're blamin' Billy for grabbin' as the same things you want. A change. Excitement. Fun."

Disregarding him, she wept on. "He can go to the hotel or he can ride off into the hills and drink booze with Mando and those crazy cowboys they hired."

Buchanan knew it was the truth. "Yeah . . . well, reckon you're right. A lady can't do the things a man can do. I don't know why. Fact is, I've known some ladies do exactly as they pleased. Kinda crazy ladies. But they enjoyed theirselves, I'll say that. Maybe you ought to try it."

"Try it? Try what?"

"Well, you could ride out to the graze. You could go downtown and mingle with people. You could even help Miz Avery teach a Sunday-school class."

"Uncle Tom!" But she giggled. "Me, in a Sunday school?"

"Worse people have been in church.

You could even get up a sewing circle or somethin', couldn't you?"

"More like ridin' the range. Or even drinkin' in the hotel with those people. But I purely despise those people."

Buchanan arose and picked her up under one arm. "I think you and me better get saddled up and take a ride. Clears the cobwebs."

She said, "It won't settle my problem, Uncle Tom. But I'll be glad to go with you. Anywhere at all."

"We won't go anywhere at all. I warned yawl not to go too far into the hills. Juju's people must've eaten their meat by now. They'll be hungry again, just like other folks."

They went toward the barn. The sound of Coco beating on the big bag had ceased. Now they saw him running around the perimeter of the property. Just behind him on his favorite grulla, Billy whooped and urged him on. Billy's rifle was slung in the boot and he wore a revolver in his belt.

"No Injun is going to get at Coco,"

Nora said. "Honest, if he wasn't such a dear, sweet person I'd be jealous of him. My baby and my husband are crazy about him."

Buchanan told her sharply, "Coco is a good friend to have. You should be grateful that Coco loves yawl."

"Oh, I am . . . I am." She grabbed a saddle and started for the stall of her little red pony, shouldering it like a man. "It's me. I'm mad at me, I guess."

Buchanan saddled Nightshade, letting Nora work out some of her frustration on the pony, which didn't like bridles too much. Then they led the horses into the yard and he said to her, "Looks like Billy's havin' so much fun, what say we join him?"

She was fighting the pony into submission. She could ride as well as any of the *vaqueros* on the plains. She was a fine little lady, Buchanan's almost-adopted daughter. He laughed at her and they rode out helter skelter, even Nightshade getting into the notion of it, frisking and cavorting as they chased Coco and

Billy around the edge of the big Billy Button property.

Juju, on a scout, lay low and looked on. He saw the black man running and thought he was trying to escape. He grew quite excited about it, thinking of some way to help. Then he realized it was all in fun, because there were Buchanan and the mother of the baby joining in and the black man waving at them and grinning. Maybe it was some kind of a strange game. The white-eyes played a lot of games.

It was not a time for games. The young men were still apart, doing whatever they had in mind to do. The older men were getting hungry again. It was a difficult world when a man hungered so often and so quickly, he thought. He could go without food for a long, long time himself, if he had water. But there was no quieting the others with this telling; they could not do it, which was one of the reasons he was the chief and could take a Mexican wife to the exclusion of others, defying local custom.

At that, he was not so proud of the distinction. He had seen several young squaws on the reservation before they had come out on this expedition, very succulent and quite ready to wed a strong chieftan. But if he so much as mentioned that one son was scarcely enough for a leader Emalita would fly into a fit. He was not afraid of the tribe nor the white-eyes or anyone in the world excepting Emalita. He retreated now, leaving Buchanan and friends to their crazy game and went to an appointed place near the encampment but where the other braves could not see nor hear and there Emalita awaited him.

"What did you learn?" she asked, confident that he had not failed.

"They play games. We starve and they are planning a fiesta. The black man and the big man called Mac are to meet. Fight to the finish, someone said. They are wagering back and forth. Many people will come to Encinal."

"Many people? For the fiesta?"

"Yes." He paused, then said, "Jo-san was in the town."

"You saw him?"

"No. He stole food. I would have got to it before he did, but I listened to the talk in the cantina, where I learned about the fiesta. Then it was too late."

"Buchanan?"

"Yes. Buchanan was there, reading track."

"Then he knows about Jo-san?"

"He knows. Buchanan reads track as we do."

"Will he send people after Jo-san?"

"No. But he will be ready for anything that we try."

"Then we cannot steal the baby?"

"Not unless it is on the day of the fiesta and they grow careless at their games. Then we could try it."

She said thoughtfully, "Then Buchanan would bring us food and guns and ammunition. Yes. But he would also bring us terrible trouble."

"We will have to take that gamble," said Juju sadly.

190

"Remember, Buchanan is not a friend. He is a man with brains, but he is not one of us."

"True," she agreed. But Buchanan was one of *her* race, she thought privately. She had Spanish ancestors, she was a white woman. She knew Buchanan better than did Juju or any other Indian, she believed.

Juju said, "I think it better we do not talk of anything but the fiesta to the others."

"Yes. They can take heart if they think we can steal into town during a fiesta and get what we need."

"Good," he grunted. They walked to the encampment, Emalita two steps behind, the perfect squaw to all outward appearances.

6

BY midweek they were pouring into Encinal from anywhere and everywhere. The news that a fight was actually authorized and legalized by the territory spread like a prairie fire through the western country. They came from Montana and Wyoming and Texas and Arizona and Colorado, and they came from San Francisco, and a whole trainload from Chicago switched to several hired stages. Most of them knew Coco Bean and Buchanan. An amazing number knew Big Jim McMillan.

A gambling man from Fort Worth said to Buchanan, "Yawl may have bit off a big chaw, there, Tom. I seen this McMillan beat two nigras in one night. Next week he took on one of them travelin' champs. Fella hit Mac a hundred punches, never budged him. Mac won a decision and a big purse."

"I wonder why he don't work at it, if he's so good?" Buchanan pondered.

The man looked around the crowded saloon of the hotel and lowered his voice. "Word gets around. Seems like he might have another name. Seems like he was caught in a bank one night, after hours."

"A bank, you said?"

"Just a rumor," the gambler said. "But it had a solid sound. And the little lady there, you know her?"

"Heloise Beaumont?"

The man winked. "Name of Dare. Married to, or livin' with, the feller she says is her brother. An old game, y'know?"

Buchanan said, "Wouldn't say I'm surprised. She owns the hotel, though. Had some cash when she got here."

"Right. She always is able to earn some cash." The wink was more pronounced. "Laid a little cash on her myself a couple times, know what I mean?"

Buchanan said, "She's played it pretty straight here. Maybe she wants to quit, like every floozie I ever knew. Or said they did."

"Most *say* they want to quit." The gambler shrugged. "But she's making hay while this sun shines, no argument about that. The bar alone is a gold mine, the prices she's chargin'. Know where I can get a bottle at the right price?"

"Jake Stein's general store," Buchanan told him. "Tell your friends—if any."

"A gambler's got no friends. How much you bettin' on your nigra?"

"He ain't my nigra, he's my friend," said Buchanan for the thousandth time, it seemed to him. "I got about every two-bit piece I own on him."

"I heard you bet a heap Coco'd knock him out. That's the money I'd like to get at."

"Too late," said Buchanan. He had started to feel uncomfortable some time before, when the wise men began grabbing his wagers on a knockout. He and Coco could both go broke if McMillan had the iron jaw everyone spoke about so highly.

The gambling man went off to the faro layout. Heloise had hired a couple of traveling dealers. They were playing it square all the way, Buchanan knew. She was too smart to make a bad play among all these sharp members of the gambling society.

She was working the bar, occasionally buying a drink, getting the suckers a bit drunk and sending them to the tables befuddled. Beaumont wore his marshal's star prominently displayed, shined bright for the occasion. He was satisfied to act as greeter and puissant lawman for the out of towners. Daggett watched the bar and the cash drawer, working the itinerant bartenders in shifts to keep them on their toes.

Hamilton Mizer conducted tours of his properties every morning and afternoon. He drove the prospective buyers himself, hiring the rig. Chatterton seemed to be in on the real estate deals with him. They actually disposed of some properties and were highly excited about the future of the "great city of Encinal."

Jake Stein and the other merchants did a land office business. The hotel was filled early and every citizen with a spare bedroom—and some without—took in a visitor.

Billy Button could scarcely restrain his excitement and enthusiasm at the holiday air of the town, when Buchanan sent him in. Finally he had the clever idea of putting up a tent. He had it brought over from Silver, where a circus had gone broke. The roustabouts, stranded, came with it, bringing their cots, and Billy acquired many more here and there, as far away as El Paso. He charged four bits per head per night. The weather held good, and there was never an empty mattress by the middle of the week. Now he had an excuse to be in town every day and some nights.

Buchanan remained as much as possible with Coco and Nora and Teresa and the baby. They held down the home hearth. Not that Nora was happy.

Billy didn't notice. He had put up a heavy canvas wall, which cut off a third of the tent, and there were soon plenty of ladies to rent those cots. He hired two local boys to stand guard and patrolled the area himself to maintain some kind of order. The ladies were not averse to male companionship, but Billy was determined they should not entertain beneath his canvas. It wasn't that he minded a bit, but he knew Miz Avery and several other ladies of the Encinal Holy Church had their eyes on him. He could not afford to make enemies of them—he wanted his son to be christened and he wanted to wear the mantle of semirespectability at least.

Hamilton Mizer paused one day to congratulate him. "Enterprise. That is what makes success for young men," the banker said. "You don't need the income, either. Very good thinking. You are reminding your clients that their money is safe in the bank, are you not?"

"They're all makin' bets. You're holdin' all the stakes," said Billy. "Nothin' better happen to the bank, Mr. Mizer."

"Nothing can happen. I have hired certain men to guard it, even while the fight is taking place on Saturday," said Mizer loftily. "Nothing can prevent the success of this—er—sales opportunity. Everyone is making money it seems—excepting your friend, Buchanan."

"I wouldn't worry about Uncle Tom," Billy said, scowling.

"No offense, no offense," Mizer said and walked away.

Uncle Tom was somewhat of a disappointment. So many people knew him, or had heard of him, he might have been the center of attention during the gala days prior to the big event. He came into town rarely and then for brief moments when he stood at the bar in the Palace Hotel and viewed the festivities with detached amusement.

Now, as Mizer vanished in the direction of the bank, Heloise approached. She was accompanied by a woman a foot taller than she. Billy touched his hat.

Heloise said, "Billy Button, this heah is Bea Johnson. She is a friend of mine, a deah friend. Have you got a place for her in youah fine establishment heah?"

Bea Johnson wore the tightest dress Billy had ever seen. It seemed to melt into a statuesque figure that defied description. She was all bosoms and narrow waist and shapely hips. She smiled upon Billy, secure in the knowledge of her appeal to all men.

Billy said, "How do, Miz Johnson. I'm sorry, but every last corner is filled, Miss Heloise. I'm plumb sorry."

"Oh, now that is too bad." Heloise clapped her strong little hands together. "But wait. Supposin' I bring over a bed from our storage room? Could you squeeze it in?"

"You can look for yourself." He stepped aside. The two boys were cleaning the tent, making up the beds. It was very neat and orderly. Heloise and the large lady exclaimed over it.

Then Miss Johnson spoke. She had a deep voice that emanated from the full chest with musical power. "Mr. Button, I'll pay five dollars per day for a place to

199

rest my weary head. I came all the way from St. Louis to see this bout. I want to get down a bet or two on Coco Bean to beat this McMillan."

"She just won't listen to reason," said Heloise. "I think there's a spot in that corner, honey, if we just move this cot . . . and this one heah. Now, ain't that fine? I'll send the bed over right away."

She had, indeed, rearranged things so that the bed would fit. Billy scratched his head. "Maybe I shoulda had you as pardner here. But I hear you're doin' all the business you need."

"Without any help from you," said Heloise sadly. "You have deserted us, haven't you? Just because Griff and Dolan were crooks—must you hold that against me, really?"

"I been busy," Billy claimed. "First with Coco. Then with this here—uh—enterprise."

Bea Johnson said, "And I hear you don't even let the gals have their friends in."

"It ain't that kind of town," Billy

explained. Then he asked, "How come you're bettin' on Coco, Miz Johnson?"

The handsome lady smiled. She spoke softly. "Coco is an old and dear friend of mine. I know how good he is."

"Well, then, you better come out to our house before you do anything else," Billy said. "Coco's trainin' there. Maybe . . . you come on with me. We'll see. Heloise, I'll hire the bed from you, fifty cents per night. Okay?"

"And make four-fifty on my friend, Bea?"

"No friend of Coco's pays any money to me," said Billy loftily. "Could be Nora'll ask Miss Johnson to stay at our place. We got a couch she could have for nothin'."

He beckoned, going to where the team of matched bays awaited his bidding. He was replacing the bridles when he suddenly realized what he had done.

Heloise cried, "Oh, how nice of yawl! It's the first time, Bea, I do declare, that I've been invited!"

He opened his mouth to protest but it

was too late. His natural enthusiasm and hospitality had got him in real trouble this time. There was no way he could tell Heloise that her friend from St. Louis was welcome but that she was not.

The carriage was black with red wheels, highly polished since it was Billy's pride and joy. The bays were spirited, arching their necks as if they knew they were not ordinary horse flesh. Billy gave Heloise a hand and she hopped into the rear seat, clapping and chortling. It was a bit different with the Johnson lady; the dress was very tight. He blinked and turned bright red as the skirt slid up above her knees when she clambered in beside her friend.

They drove down Main Street, and the little boys whistled and marched with knees high in imitation of the team of bays. Men grinned and a few laughed openly. Hamilton Mizer stood in the door of the bank and stared disapprovingly as the carriage wended its way to the Button dwelling.

They were all on the veranda. Coco had

been tapering off, working less each day, having neared peak form. He held the baby on his lap. Teresa was serving lemonade from a tray. Nora was fanning herself, and Buchanan was seated on the steps, long legs outstretched. The carriage pulled into the driveway, came around in front of the house, and stopped.

For a moment no one moved. Then Buchanan was on his feet, going to the rescue.

"Miss Beaumont . . ." He paused.

Coco was peering, shading his eyes. He leaned forward so far he almost fell on his face. Then he said, "Miz Bea Johnson, as I live and breathe." He started to roar with laughter. Then he covered his mouth and stifled himself.

Billy said, "Uh—I better put up the team until I—we—uh—need 'em. I mean . . . I better . . ."

Buchanan was handing down the ebullient Heloise, who slapped hands and marched up on the veranda and said, "Miz Button, you just got to meet my friend from St. Louis. Miz Johnson, this is Miz Button. It would be so wonderful if you got a place for her to stay. Just like Southe'n hospitality always was, bless you!"

Nora said, "Miss Johnson, how do you do." She was completely at a loss. She did not know whether to be angry or polite.

Coco had reached up and taken hold of Miss Johnson. He set her down as easily as if she had been a hogshead of whiskey. He said in a hoarse whisper, "You still got the house?"

"Oh, no," said Bea Johnson. "I sold it. Lookin' around for a new place. Heard about the fight, knew I could win a bet on you. Maybe this town needs a good house."

"For the Lord," Coco said earnestly. "Don't you say one word about such a thing in this place. In this town! For the Lord!"

"For the Lord? Or for you? Is that Buchanan, that big fella?"

"That's Tom Buchanan. And don't let him know you had a place in St. Looey."

"It was the fanciest house in town!"

"The fanciest fancy house," said Coco. "Just don't mention it around here."

She winked at him. "Okay, partner. Mum's the word. Now gimme an intro to that big rascal, Buchanan. Personal-like. Ya know what I mean?"

"Oh, me. You goin' to try your tricks on Tom Buchanan? Lordy me, Bea. Lordy me!"

"Don't call on strangers when neighbors are near," she said, taking his arm and steering him toward Buchanan.

Billy was still fussing with the team behind the house. Nora was listening to the prattle of the baby, concealing her annoyance as best she could. Teresa got up and took the baby into the house.

Coco was saying to Buchanan, "This here is a lady I knowed in St. Looey. She bet on all my fights. I like to win her a fortune, truly I did. She cut me in. A real nice lady."

Buchanan said, "Nice to meet you, Miz Johnson."

"Bea," she said. "Call me Bea—I never

sting a pal. You sure are a big one, Buchanan."

"You're not exactly a midget yourself." He grinned at her. She had cheeks a bit too pink to be true, but her teeth were white and even and there was a dimple in her left cheek. Her eyes were dark and wise. "You mind bein' a big gal?"

"Not a bit," she retorted. "And I purely like a big guy." She looked around, went on, "Seems like a nice right joint the kids have here. That little fella, he made a bloomer bringin' us out here, didn't he?"

"That's all accordin'," Buchanan said frankly.

She took his arm, rested her bosom upon it. "Why doncha show me the premises, big boy, and tell me accordin' to what?"

He hesitated, then called, "Nora, I'm going to show Miz Johnson around."

"See if you can find Billy," she replied.

They both walked around to the rear of the house. Billy was pretending to fuss with the harness he kept in perfect order at all times. Buchanan fixed him with a hard gaze and jerked a thumb. Billy blinked, swallowed hard, then began a slow, trudging walk to the battleground on the veranda.

Bea Johnson said, "He is kinda cute, at that. Know all about him, do ya?"

"Enough."

She said, "Heloise tryin' to work him?"

"Heloise was doin' same."

"Yeah. She just can't help it. Coco said I should keep my yap shut, but I know I can tell you. Had a house in St. Louis. Best in the damn state. She stayed awhile, bein' broke. Then she got lucky and made a stake and picked up with that fella, that sissified Beaumont."

"Sissified?" He shook his head. "He's more like a snake. Lays low and quiet, strikes when ready."

"Could be," she said. "Anyway, Coco told me to lay off. This ain't the town. Right?"

"Right. Anyway, it wouldn't support a classy house. They got a pig ranch out a ways for the cowboys and miners."

She said, "Now, it's okay to be friends. Right?"

"Sure, why not?" He liked her. Whatever her profession she had an open, cleancut manner of speaking. He imagined she was one of the square-shooting kind—he had met them before up and down the frontier, women who found no means of support but refused to do menial labor or marry anyone who'd have them. Some were bad, some indifferent and dull. The others were like Bea Johnson.

She said, "The little fella about offered me a couch to sleep on. No dice, huh?"

"There's no couch in the house big enough for you."

"I get it," she said, smiling at him. "Tell me, is there an angle to this fight of Coco's?"

"You ever know Coco to have an angle?"

"Not his, the darlin'. No—I mean who's got the ax ready?"

"When did you get into town?" They

walked past the carriage house and around the back of the barn.

"This mornin'," she told him. "I know that McMillan. He's a horse."

"Uh-huh," said Buchanan. "I'm bettin' Coco kayoes him."

"You are? How much?"

"All I got."

"But there's plenty of McMillan money around. Therefore and positively, big boy, there's an angle."

"I kinda doubt it. I mean, the fight is on the level, and lots of people think McMillan can win—or at least get a draw. Beaumont's the referee but I'll be in Coco's corner and there'll be no fudgin'."

"But outside the fight, you think there's somethin'?"

"That's about it."

She said, "I heard somethin' about that McMillan. Like he done some time. For safe crackin'. He's a big blowup guy, they whisper. You heard that?"

"No." His mind went again to the bank where all the stake money and much other cash was being held. But McMillan would be in the ring . . .

She said, "Freddy Daggett, he's another cutie. Picks a neat pocket, you know?"

"Daggett? He seems a well-educated bloke," Buchanan said. "One of them from the East."

"Yeah. And slick-fingered. Heloise has got a great bunch around her. Y' know, big boy, she ain't really too smart."

"She's smart enough."

"Just about. She thinks she's *real* clever, though, and that's her problem. She talks too much. Tried to sell me a piece of her hotel this afternoon."

"On the strength of today's business?"

"Yeah. Am I that dumb-lookin'? The fight's drawin' in the crowd, right?"

He answered, "And she's got a mortgage. Matter of fact if Coco wins I'll be holdin' it over the hotel."

"You bettin' that way?"

"All the way."

She said, "I'll sleep in the tent. There's a corner I can squeeze into."

"Tell you what," Buchanan said. "Billy's got a real bathroom in the house. Nora would let a friend of mine use it."

She said, "You're plenty smart, big boy. You even know when a gal would give a lot for a decent bath."

"If you just got in this mornin', and you been travelin' on a stage—any dummy would know you need a bath, a lady like you."

She gave him a long glance below veiled lids. "I declare, big boy, if it was somewheres else I'd ask you to gimme a hand and scrub my back."

"And I'd be real proud to take you up," he said. "Let's go and talk to Nora before she kills Heloise dead."

They found the situation on the veranda practically unchanged. Coco and Billy sat silent. Nora listened and Heloise chattered like a magpie.

"I do declare, this is the nicest place." She clapped her hands. "I do wish someone asked me to stay at such a fine house as this."

Bea Johnson did not alter expression.

211

"If Mr. Button would be so good, I'd like to get back. That bed must be delivered from the hotel by now, mustn't it, Heloise?"

"Why . . . why . . ." Heloise gulped and changed courses. "Of course, honey. I mean, if you really . . ."

"I really." Bea Johnson bowed toward Nora, and Billy scuttled off to fetch the carriage. "So pleased to make your acquaintance. This is one swell joint you got here. Hope you 'preciate it. Not many gals have it so swell."

"Thank you," said Nora. "I guess I do appreciate it."

Heloise had recovered her aplomb. "Well, it is scrumptious. And too bad you don't want Bea to sleep here a few nights."

"I wasn't asked," said Nora. The storm warning was up now for all to see. Two pink spots were on her cheeks.

Heloise smiled upon Billy. "The ladies do have their say, don't they now, Billy darlin'? Should've known. Man's married, he toes the mark. Walks the line? Ha, ha, ha."

Nora said to her, "You wouldn't know, would you? A single lady like you."

Bea Johnson cleared her throat. "It's been a real pleasure." She shook her head emphatically at Buchanan as he started to speak. "I'll borrow your hotel bathroom, Heloise. Like to get clean. So-long, big boy, see you around sometime."

Buchanan watched them go. She had started a train of thought in his mind. Daggett, a pickpocket, a man clever with his hands. And he was remaining in town, skipping the fight to attend the bar and watch over Heloise.

Watch over Heloise? Now that was wasted time and motion, Buchanan thought. Heloise needed about as much protection as . . . as . . . Emalita of the Juju bunch.

Dolan and Griff, he thought, could not be far away. He had never believed for a moment that Heloise had been serious in banishing them. They were useful to her and she would never let a man go if she could use him.

So that made three men. The town would be deserted. Mizer had hired guards, men who hung around the saloons and picked up odd jobs. They would be of no use.

On the other hand there was the sturdy vault . . .

But McMillan was a dynamite man. It kept coming back to that. A fellow clever with his hands could learn a lot in a very short time.

The fight, he thought, was the thing. McMillan was very fast on his feet. He was a boxer. He would keep the bout going for as long as possible, hoping to wear down Coco and win after an exhausting hour or two of battling.

The key, he thought, was the fight. And he had to be there to second Coco and watch out for shenanigans, And everyone else would be there, even the marshal of Encinal.

Lost in thought, he found himself walking down to the road. He shook himself back to the present and returned, skirting the circular driveway, going toward the rear of the house. Coco was waiting for him and he knew something was wrong by the stubbornness of the fighter's chin.

Coco said, "We're leavin'."

"Leaving? Who's leaving what?"

"Me and the baby and Teresa and Nora, that's who is leavin'."

"I see," He saw it, indeed. He knew there was no way to fight it. "Better take the buggy, hook up that gray. It'll crowd you a little but best get away before Billy comes home and there's a big fuss."

"You ain't goin' to put in your two-bits worth?"

"Who, me? I didn't bring Heloise Beaumont out here."

"You played up to that whore-lady."

"Whore-lady? Hell, Coco, she's your old friend from St. Louis. You announced it."

Coco waved his huge fists. "You think I could say what she was in front of Nora and Teresa? And all? How could I do that?"

"She don't look like a whore-lady to me," Buchanan said. "You sure about her?"

"She run the biggest house in St. Looey!"

"Oh!" said Buchanan, pretending vast relief. "That's different. That don't make her a whore. Just the gals that work for her."

"What's the difference?" Coco demanded. "You know that Billy's got 'em down there in that tent. I bet she come to run the place for him."

"That's where you're wrong," Buchanan told him. "Billy has been runnin' that place on the level."

"You tell that to Nora!"

She was coming out of the house, carrying the baby. Teresa was loaded down with a carpetbag and a valise. Coco ran to relieve her of the burden and to pick up a portable baby bath. Coco and Teresa headed directly for the stable.

Nora paused to look at Buchanan, reproach in her swimming eyes.

Buchanan said, "I swear I never knew she was a madame. She seems a right nice lady to me."

"Never mind her," Nora said in a low, tragic voice. "He brought that Beaumont woman here. He actually brought her onto my veranda."

"Well, I reckon he was stuck, bringin' Coco's friend and all. So he made a mistake."

"You should back him up. That's his trouble. He tries to imitate you. He can't do it because he's nothin' but a bigmouth little pipsqueak. He struts around and . . . and . . . I won't live with him a day longer. I won't!"

"It's goin' to make a lot of folks satisfied if not happy, y' know," Buchanan said. "People love seein' the mighty fall. You two are the luckiest couple in town even if you don't know it, and there's plenty folks hate the lucky."

"I don't care about folks any more 'n I ever did," she cried. "And you know well enough that's nothin'. Zero! Let 'em talk. Let 'em rave. I'm goin' back to my own place."

"Uh-huh." Buchanan was out of his element. This was an experience brand new to him. There was nothing he could think of that would help. Then he saw that Coco had put his carpetbag outside the back door. He yelled, "Coco! Are you going with them? Are you really leavin' here?"

"I sure am," Coco called back from the stable. "Just as soon as I harness this hoss and can load the buggy. Yawl can't treat my baby and my ladies like of this!"

Buchanan said, "Your trainin'! You'll lose your edge, man! This is no good for you with the fight comin' up in a few days."

"Huh! You and that bigmouth Billy worry about the fight. I ain't goin' to."

Buchanan took off his hat and mopped his brow. When Coco talked to him like this, he had come to a pretty pass. He could have sworn he was innocent of wrongdoing, but his best friend and the little girl he loved believed that he had. Furthermore there was no way he could plead innocent, get on his knees, attempt to convince them that they were wrong.

"Wait 'til I get hold of that Billy," he groaned to himself as Coco brought out the buggy. He watched them crowd into the narrow vehicle. They really needed the carriage to transport them and their luggage. But of course Billy had the carriage, which made them martyrs, suffering for their elevated principles. He could see it all and in a way he could understand it.

But in no way could he figure how to straighten it out. They drove off without another glance in his direction. It was the first falling out with Coco that had ever occurred. He thought about Nora and what she had said. If Billy was indeed only trying to imitate Tom Buchanan, then there was something wrong—something wrong with both of them, maybe.

He went into the kitchen. Teresa always had a cold platter set for him. He rummaged in the newfangled ice box and found it. He was eating steadily through chicken and cold beans and buttered bread when Billy drove in. He put the dish in the sink and went out to the stable.

Billy said, "Where's ev'body? Didn't see anyone comin' in the drive."

Buchanan said, "They're gone."

"Gone? Gone where?"

Buchanan moved to help unharness the bays. "Back to the little house."

"What? What the hell are you tryin' to tell me, Uncle Tom?" Billy came running around the back of the carriage.

"Nora and Coco didn't take kindly to you nor me and the two women and whatever," Buchanan told him. "Like you shouldn't have brought 'em out here. Especially Heloise."

"I can explain about that. I was bein' polite to Miz Johnson, who is Coco's friend. Right?"

"Miz Johnson used to run a whorehouse in St. Louis," said Buchanan lugubriously. "Me, I thought she was a right nice lady. Still do."

Billy reeled against the rear wheel of the carriage, bug-eyed. "You mean I . . . we . . . oh brother! Oh, me!"

Buchanan said, "They don't like us right now. Nora, Coco, Teresa—and I wouldn't be surprised the baby."

Billy's voice was weak. "Uncle Tom, what we goin' to do?"

"Tell you the truth, I haven't got the slightest notion," Buchanan answered frankly.

"But my wife! And my baby!"

"It's a tough one, all right. But I wouldn't expect they're gone forever. The old Mulligan house ain't that far away."

"It's far enough!"

"If they started for El Paso, now, or San Francisco, or—"

"Don't talk like that! We got to do somethin', Uncle Tom."

"Looks like I ain't the one to give advice." Buchanan was honestly humble, "Nora says the trouble is that you been tryin' to imitate me. And I ain't the best example for a married man to follow."

"There ain't nothin' wrong with bein'

like you! Doggone it, she's got no right! You're the best man I ever knew!" There were tears in Billy's eyes. "Maybe I been wrong, hangin' around the hotel, lettin' Heloise make over me. But when you found out she was crooked, I stayed away. Didn't I? How did I know Coco's friend was a madame? How'd we know that?"

"Sure. But when people get their mad up, they don't care much if you're innocent. Seen people lynched because of that kind of mad. Might's well admit we shouldn't have been so pleasant and friendly to Heloise and Miz Johnson."

"But it's just good manners!"

"You rather be good-mannered or have your wife and baby and a champion prizefighter who might louse up this match by stickin' away and not trainin' right?"

"Oh, Lord! I hadn't thought of that yet," groaned Billy. "The tent. Those kids ain't to be trusted too much. I got to eat and go down and—"

Buchanan said, "I'll check your tent. And keep an eye on your pal Heloise."

"I didn't want to bring her out here. She foxed me."

"You foxed yourself, Billy. It ain't any use cryin' over spilt milk. That's true. But you have been actin' the fool. You been stayin' away from home. You got to admit you're wrong before you can even start gettin' back with Nora. That's the way I see it."

"I'll do anything. This ain't right. This house—it's nothin' without Nora and the baby."

"Keep that in mind." He felt sorry for the little fellow. It was a bad time, and he didn't know any way to make it better.

7

THE whole town was talking. But luckily, Buchanan thought, walking down Main Street the day before the big fight, there were now so many strangers around, and the excitement had mounted to such heights, that it was not ruinous to Nora and Billy and their future in Encinal. If they could get it fixed between them everything might work out in the end. Not that he had thought up any ideas how it could be mended.

The betting was all on McMillan now. Coco had been seen puttering around the old Mulligan house, running errands, tending the garden, playing with the baby. He had not been seen training. He had not been up to the carriage house to strike the heavy bag. Every day the tall, wide figure of McMillan was highly visible running and shadowboxing and snorting and knocking down anyone who dared put on the gloves with him.

Bea Johnson met Buchanan at the big tent. She said, "Thanks for comin' down, big boy. I sure am sorry about the trouble."

"I'm sorry you didn't get to use the bath," he said. "What did you want to see me about?"

"Coco Bean."

"I can't tell you anything."

"Can't? Or won't?"

"Can't."

She said, "They're givin' odds, now, y' know."

"I heard."

"Heloise is takin' all the credit for runnin' Coco off."

"I heard."

"You and me, we stand to lose our shirts."

He looked her over, grinning. She wore another of the tight costumes out of which she seemed about to burst. "You wearin' a shirt, lady?"

"You could make that your business,

big boy," she replied, rolling her eyes. She made a joke of it, a pleasant exchange.

"My turn to ask. You heard anything that might help?"

She grew serious on the instant. "No. But it stands to reason, don't it?"

He said, "Dynamite. Quick hands. The bank. Maybe I oughta stay in town. Let Coco fight it out."

"And lose?"

He sighed. "It could happen. If he don't see me in his corner he might get rattled."

She said, "The gals are goin' to the fight. First time. Nobody can stop 'em, right?"

"There'll be some scandal."

"Who cares?"

He eyed her. "Not me. You sure you don't know anything?"

"Nope. I don't *know*. But, like you, I can guess, big boy."

He grunted. "Be seein' you around."

She nodded. "I'll bet on that."

He walked back to Main Street. Local

people looked dubiously at him and he knew they had bet on Coco. The sharpsters and gamblers laughed at him. Hamilton Mizer rubbed his hands as if they itched, standing in the doorway to the bank. Buchanan stopped.

"Better hire a couple extra guards for tomorrow," he suggested. "Lot of money in the safe, there. More 'n you can afford to lose."

"I already hired my help," Mizer told him. "Just you see to it that your man shows up. If he is your man."

"He's his own man. And he'll show." Buchanan went on down the street and then up to the big house on the hill. Billy Button sat on the steps of the veranda, whittling. There was a pile of shavings at his feet. He was disconsolate.

Buchanan said, "Nothin' new that I could find. Got to get off my hunches."

"Nora won't even talk to me," Billy said.

Buchanan said, "There's all kinds of liquor bein' sold in town, all kinds of gamblin' going on. The gals are makin' a

227

good dollar, too. You and Coco certainly set the town up for the gold rush."

"I know it." Billy's voice was mournful. "I been a damn fool. Sittin' here I can see it all. That lookin' glass thing in the bar, I never woulda seen it if you hadn't set into the game. I let Heloise twist me around her finger." He brightened a bit. "At least I never did fall for that brother of hers."

Buchanan hesitated, then said, "Hate to sink another knife into you, Billy. She ain't his sister. They just travel together, cheatin' and stealin'."

Billy sat for a long moment, staring straight ahead. "Come to think of it, if she ain't a Southerner—and he is—they couldn't be brother and sister now, could they? You done told me that long ago."

Buchanan said, "Just so you keep it in mind. Because tomorrow you and me, we go to the fight. Early."

"You think Coco wants you in his corner?"

"We'll know tomorrow."

Billy said, "Half the town'll be broke

if Coco don't win. Reckon we'll have to leave."

"Sufficient unto the day," Buchanan said. "Let's get ourselves somethin' to eat."

"You do that. I just ain't got any appetite." Billy returned to his whittling.

In the back office private to herself and her cohorts Heloise sat and sipped at whiskey. Her cheeks were flushed and her eyes sparkled. She clapped her hands together.

"Tomorrow night we'll all be rich!"

Elton Beaumont shifted his weight, looked at Freddy Daggett. "One slip and we're all in the soup."

Daggett said coolly, "There won't be a slip. Griff and Dolan are all set. They've been out of circulation so long they're raring to go."

"They'd better bring the loot over here before they rare!" Beaumont said.

"I'll be with them," Daggett said, staring at Beaumont.

Heloise cut in sharply. "If they didn't

229

bring it here—we'd have Buchanan and everyone on them. And Elton would lead the posse and see that they were shot before they could talk out of line, too."

"They won't renege," Daggett said. "I'll be blowing up the vault. I'll be in charge. They will merely knock out the guards and stand watch."

"And help carry the money over here," Beaumont insisted.

"Of course. And I'll be here to hide it," Heloise said.

They were silent, thinking it all over. Griff and Dolan had not been discovered in the mine shaft; they had only to lie low until they could be extricated. A little time and the whole thing would be blown over, Heloise thought. She could sell the hotel. She had taken in a lot of money— the bank loot would be enough to take her to Europe for a stay. She had thoughts of making a marriage—a duke or a count, perhaps. Wealthy American women could marry titles at will, she had heard.

Beaumont said, "One more thing. That Johnson woman, your friend from St.

Louis. She's been asking a hell of a lot of questions around town."

"And getting no answers," said Heloise. "I know that."

"Well, she might get in the way."

"I have no compunction about scragging a woman," Daggett said. "Stop worrying, Elton, please?"

"I'll be out there in that ring, sweating. I've got to see that the fight keeps going long enough for you to operate. It may not be easy."

"Mac will make it easy," said Heloise. "He will dance and dance. He calls it waltzin'. He'll waltz the nigra around and around."

"He'd better," said Freddy Daggett. "Blowing the vault will take a bit of time. Then the escape, the ride out of town. Getting rid of the masks. Then the circling back to town. A bit of time."

"It will all work out," said Heloise. "You just go about your business as though all was as usual. Let me do the worrying."

They both went out. They had many

things on their minds. Heloise tipped the whiskey bottle. She went back to her dreams of grandeur.

Juju moved like a phantom, going from one clump of brush to another, from rock to rock. He made no sound, climbing the slope above the mine shaft. When he had gained a vantage point he stood up and made the sound of a bird call. Emalita came up to him, more slowly, but with as much skill.

Juju said, "Behold. Your son."

The five young Apaches were huddled around a small, smokeless, flameless fire. Emalita looked down upon them and said, "I think they are as hungry as we are."

Juju said. "The great hunter has found no more than we old folks. Let us go down."

They went down the hillside. Jo-san leaped to his feet but the others scarcely moved.

Juju said, "So. You have not eaten."

"We have eaten," said Jo-san.

"But not lately," Emalita noted.

"I stole food from the town."

"We know," said Juju. "We know about everything. Except, great leader, why do you linger here?"

Jo-san said, "You will know."

"And will I care?"

"You will have food and guns and bullets. You will have everything money can buy," Jo-san promised.

"And when will this glorious event happen?"

"Tomorrow. Tomorrow certain things will happen. We, my men and I, we will be ready."

"And you don't want to tell us about it?" asked Emalita. "You do not need any help?"

"I need nothing save that you leave me alone," said Jo-san.

Juju said, "Enough. Come, woman."

They went away, melting into the night, leaving the youths to their own devices. They walked across the foothills and to within sight of the town of Encinal. They sat on their heels and talked together.

"A young fool," said Juju.

"Yes." Emalita lifted a shoulder. "Mine. And yours."

"Yes. Now, when all is taking place among the white-eyes tomorrow and Buchanan is busy, we take the woman and the baby."

"It is the only sensible thing to do," she agreed.

"Buchanan will pay anything for them. Guns, bullets, meat . . . anything."

"Yes," she said. "And death, too, if they are harmed."

Juju was silent for a moment. Then he said slowly, "There comes a time, woman, when a man loses fear. I cannot go through life afraid of Buchanan. This time if he gets in the way . . . I shall kill him."

She did not reply. She looked down at the lights of Encinal and brooded.

Buchanan awoke with the first crow of the yard rooster. It was overcast when he went to use the bathroom, to shave and dress in his best dark blue shirt, his crimson silk kerchief, his tapered town pants that fit into his hand-tooled boots.

He went downstairs and Billy was, amazingly, already in the kitchen. He was wearing black—shirt, pants, boots, even his hat, which hung on a peg near the door. His expression matched the somber hue. He was scrambling eggs. A rasher of bacon was already sizzling on the stove.

Buchanan said, "Cheer up. The worst is yet to come."

"I know. That's what's got me about bustin'. You reckon she'll stay home with the baby?"

Buchanan said, "Nope."

"Me neither. She's goin' to take the buggy and see Coco fight. She ain't goin' to miss it, no matter what Miz Avery might say."

"Best we shouldn't think about that," Buchanan suggested. "Best we should get straight just what we are doin'."

"We go out and survey the land where the fight's takin' place. We make sure there ain't anything funny about the ropes. We bring our own water bottle and our own water. We check the sun and how it'll shine at four o'clock when the fight starts."

"We find a place close by for our horses."

"Yeah," Billy said. "The horses. Somebody might try to spook the horses."

"That's your job. Nightshade don't spook. How about your grulla?"

"He'll shy off from noise or anything flappin'."

"You got another horse?"

Billy said, "One of the bays. But he ain't too saddle broke. I mean, that's a young team but Toby, he stands for anything. Holds Nell down all the time."

"Use your judgment," Buchanan said. "And eat, boy. I can't stand to see a man starve himself."

They sat down and Billy toyed with his food. His mind was down in the little Mulligan cottage with his wife and his son. Thus it was necessary for Buchanan to clean up on the eggs, a dozen, and the bacon, a pound or so. He drank a pot of coffee and ate bread and butter and apple jelly. He felt refreshed and if he was not ready for the day, he had at least done his best to prepare.

He wore his six-gun today, against his habit when in a town. He saddled Nightshade and watched Billy bring Toby, the placid bay into the yard. He looked into the hills. He could not see them but the Apaches were up there somewhere, watching. The activity in Encinal would not escape them.

He muttered, "If we get through this and you don't misbehave too much, Juju, I'll bring more meat. I promise you."

They rode out, saw that early risers were moving in Encinal, circled around the town, back of the Palace Hotel and thus out onto the flats.

Actually the flats were undulating. The ring was set in the middle of a wide swale so that spectators could stand about and look down on the action. Buchanan paced off the distance between the stakes driven into the ground and shook his head.

"Get into town, Billy. Bring whoever

you can find that thinks he's official and bring men and a shovel."

"What's wrong?"

"The ring's to be twenty-four foot square. That's the rule. This here one is thirty feet square. It's supposed to have eight posts. They got six, leavin' room for McMillan to take his time."

Billy said, "You sure know all about it, Uncle Tom." He got onto the bay and rode for town. He wore two guns, a six-shooter and a nasty little over-and-under derringer. He was obeying every suggestion of Buchanan as though it came from the Bible. He did not know how to get back his wife and son, but he did believe it would be through his Uncle Tom. It was the only faith he maintained.

Buchanan walked around the swale. There was a sturdy bush a hundred feet from the ring. He marked it in his mind. No matter what anyone said, he meant to have the horses close during the bout. He had figured out in his mind what *might* happen. He was not certain, he had no real proof. But he believed he could figure the workings of the criminal mind. He wondered if that meant he had a crooked streak—or if he had run across so many thieves that he was beginning to think as they did.

He mounted Nightshade and rode around the perimeter of the swale. There would be space for a thousand people, and there were that many crowded into Encinal. Billy's tent had been over-crowded for three days. Men had been sleeping in their sugans all over the place. It was a wonder that Juju or Jo-san hadn't plundered a few of them, at that.

Billy was returning. Buchanan rode back to the ring, dismounted, trailed the reins. Hamilton Mizer, another early riser, and a sleepy, puffy-eyed Elton Beaumont were in a carriage drawn by livery hacks.

Buchanan asked, "Who set up this ring?"

"Why, all of us. I mean, McMillan knows about such things. Yawl are too late to complain."

Buchanan asked Billy, "You bring the shovels?"

"In the back of their carriage," Billy said. "They never saw me stick 'em in there."

Buchanan said, "Okay. Now, gentlemen, either you send people out here to put this matter straight or you stay and do the job yourselves."

Hamilton Mizer exclaimed, "I'll have you know Marshal Beaumont here is the law in Encinal."

"He won't last the day if he don't get that ring back to regulation size with eight posts in place," Buchanan said.

Beaumont swelled like a bullfrog. His face went fiery red. He put his hand on the butt of his gun and exclaimed, "Suh, you dare to talk to me like that?"

Buchanan took one huge step. His left hand descended upon Beaumont's right hand and snatched it away from the gun. His right hand described a short arc and the open palm smote the marshal alongside the head. Beaumont spun around in an arc, restrained by Buchanan's grip, his feet doing a little fandango.

Buchanan said mildly, "Billy, better take his gun before he shoots himself."

Billy stepped in and removed the marshal's gun from the holster. Hamilton Mizer was scrambling for the carriage. Billy got into his path and the banker stopped, ashen-faced, staring from Billy to Buchanan and back again.

Buchanan went on. "There comes a time when it gets serious and a man has had enough." He turned Beaumont loose so roughly the man staggered into the reluctant arms of the banker. "This prize-fight involves a heap of people and a heap of money. It's goin' to be run right. I got no objections to you as a referee, Beaumont, because a thousand people will be watchin'. You go against a mob like that and you'll hang from the nearest tree."

Beaumont gasped, spluttered. One side of his face was scarlet. Beneath it was the pallor of shock. "You . . . you . . . I am the marshal!"

"Shoot, I saw 'em hang a couple

lawmen in my time. And there was Sheriff Plummer up in Montana. You oughta read up on these matters, Beaumont. A tin badge is no good in this country. It's got to be silver. A man *earns* a silver badge."

"He was duly elected," Mizer said dimly. "He's the only law we have."

"He ain't enough. And by the way, who elected him? You and some other dimwits."

"Dimwits!" Mizer gasped protest.

"You heard right. Dimwits to elect a man like this, to let him appoint crooked deputies. It's gone far enough. You get people out here within the hour and fix this ring. You hold yourself ready to conduct this bout according to the London Prize Ring Rules."

"Who . . . who has a copy of the rules?"

Buchanan tapped his brow. "I got one. Right here. Now . . . give the man back his pistol, Billy. And you, Beaumont, try and remember never to go for it, or near it, unless you mean to shoot somebody."

Beaumont was trembling like an aspen in the wind. He tried three times to holster his gun before he succeeded. He tried to speak but there was cotton in his mouth.

Billy spoke for the first time. "Beaumont, you was plumb lucky. Supposin' Uncle Tom had drawn on you?"

Mizer seized Beaumont's arm. Together they hurried to the carriage. Billy and Buchanan watched them go.

Buchanan said, "They'll be back. I believe we need to scout around a bit. Either Juju or Jo-san has got to be in the neighborhood."

Billy asked, "You think they'd really kidnap Nora and the baby?"

"Will a thirsty horse drink clean water? It's a question of opportunity, is all. Coco has kept them away, and they knew we wasn't far off. Now would be a good time."

"How we goin' to stop 'em?" wailed Billy.

"That's what we're workin' on," said

Buchanan. "You see up yonder, where the abutment comes in from the hills?"

"I see it."

"I would guess they'll have been there. But they won't be there now."

"Why not?"

"Because they know I'll be watchin'."

They rode to the rocky hilltop, and Buchanan found marks that Billy could not possibly detect. "Okay, so they know somethin's goin' on. And there's the town . . . and the bank . . . and the general store."

Billy said, "You can't be everywheres . . . There's the men come to change the ring posts."

"We got to cover with what we got— what few people we can trust," Buchanan said.

"We should've brought the boys down from the graze."

"You wouldn't have a herd," Buchanan told him. "Juju and Jo-san both would be off for the Mex border with it."

They rode down and Buchanan spoke pleasantly to the workmen, quoting the rules at length. They listened indifferently but went to work in goodwill. Neither Mizer nor Beaumont put in an appearance.

Buchanan asked, "You gents figurin' on attendin' the fight?"

"Not me," said one. "I got no use for prizefightin'."

"Any others like you in town?"

"They'll be in the cantina."

Buchanan said, "Here's a few rounds for yawl. And take my advice, watch out for Indians."

They accepted the money, one of the last of Buchanan's ready gold coins. Then one of them said, "Let the law look after the Injuns. And eve'thing else. Encinal is gone to hell in a hack, ask me."

They took off, carrying their shovels. Buchanan shook his head.

Billy said, "They're miners. Not fighters, none of them, except with their fists, or a club."

"Juju will make Christians of them." Buchanan sighed. "Here comes the first

245

of the mob. Reckon we'll have to police it ourselves."

"Police it?"

Buchanan said, "The early birds bring their fodder. Mainly bread and cheese and . . . booze."

"You can't stop 'em from drinkin'."

"We can warn 'em that gettin' too close to the ring will get 'em swatted," Buchanan said. He picked up a stick splintered from one of the ring posts and began drawing a line in the dirt fifteen feet from the ropes. "Maybe you better empty your six-gun."

"Empty it?"

"That's what I said." Buchanan was grumpy, the responsibilities piling upon him, the possibilities of danger nagging him. "It wouldn't be nice to have it go off when you raked somebody wth the muzzle."

"Who . . . me?" Billy looked alarmed.

"You're one of the police. I'll announce it," Buchanan said. "If they don't pay attention—let 'em have it."

Billy did not answer. He was staring

toward town. Buchanan looked and was even further annoyed.

Nora was driving the buggy. Teresa had the baby. Coco sat between them, waving and bowing. The gray horse paced leisurely, and a throng of people, local adherents of Coco, surrounded the equipage and cheered. The sound of the cheering was rather remote; it sounded a lot like shouting in the dark, Buchanan thought.

Billy stood, transfixed, his heart on his sleeve. Nora ignored him, driving the buggy to the brush where Buchanan had tied up Nightshade and the grulla.

Buchanan strode to them and helped Teresa down so that Coco could descend. "You're too early," he said coldly. "Teresa . . . get back in the carriage with that kid."

Nora said sharply, "You can't tell us what to do, Uncle Tom. We're free people."

"Not here, right now, you ain't," he replied. At his harsh tone she started, bit her lip. Coco got down from the carriage.

247

He wore his tights, the American flag sash and around his shoulders a new Navajo blanket. "Turn that horse around and head him for town. And when I say get out, I want you to head straight back to Encinal in a big hurry."

"You can't . . ." She stopped. She could not face down Buchanan. She sat with her head high, face averted, as Teresa clambered back to the seat hugging Thomas Mulligan.

Fight time was approaching, and now they were all coming. There was a phalanx of women from Billy's tent. They were led by Bea Johnson. She towered over them, dressed today in white, carrying a white parasol, smiling to show her white, even teeth.

Avery was in the crowd backing Coco. He said to Buchanan, "Looks like an angel, don't she? Miz Avery'd kill her if she could get her in the sights of a gun."

"She's better than some," Buchanan growled. He went to speak with the Amazonian madame.

She said, "This is the day, big boy."

"It's the day. Can you handle the women? Keep 'em behind that line?"

"I can also handle the men," she told him. She closed the parasol. It had a shiny, sharp metal tip. "Want me to take over the shady side?"

"Split it with Billy," he said.

"You can depend on me." She fluttered her eyelids.

Buchanan finally found a smile. The woman was outrageous but she was comical. She amused him and she was useful. Nora could take lessons in tolerance from her, he thought. He went back to where Coco was walking up and down in the sun with the blanket draped over his shoulders.

"Now you're waitin' for them," Buchanan charged him. "Maybe you don't want any advice from me. If that's it—say so!"

Coco frowned. "I didn't do nothin' to you. What you hollerin' on me for?"

"You quit training. You walked off and

249

didn't get in touch. You're actin' as bad as the kids."

Coco said, "I know how to take care of myself. Nora needed me."

"You think you know. This McMillan is a fast, experienced, tough fighter. He'll try to stall you and let you wear yourself out in the sun. What about it?"

"I'll just wear him out in jig time."

Buchanan nodded. "Yes."

"You mean it?" Coco was surprised. He had been warned a dozen times not to start too fast, to conserve his energy.

"I mean it. And then you do like I say. Pronto!"

Coco asked, "You mean I should take him out quick?"

"If you can. Which I doubt. You haven't trained right. You're sweatin' while he's takin' it nice and easy."

Coco said, "Quick, huh?" He grinned. "Okay, Tom."

Buchanan said, "You remember that move we worked out a year ago?"

"I remember it."

"That's it. No other move. Just that one."

Coco said, "I remember." He resumed his pacing. The sweat was running down his face, but he made no attempt to wipe it away. He held the blanket tight around him, parading in the sun.

Now the greatest part of the crowd was arriving. In the van was Marshal Beaumont. Hamilton Mizer was there and all the sharpsters and tinhorns and wise-money men who were betting on McMillan.

And McMillan came in trotting. He towered above the crowd. He clasped his hands above his head and beamed at his reception and pranced to show how strong he was and entered the ring as Beaumont parted the ropes, then followed. Buchanan looked at Billy, who was staring hopelessly, forlornly at Nora and the baby.

Buchanan motioned to Coco, who climbed through the ropes and stood in his corner, facing outward, ignoring McMillan.

The crowd was getting too unruly. They surged toward the ring and Buchanan put up his hand, going to the center position, overshadowing Beaumont. Billy started, then took up his patrol of two sides of the ring, motioning people back of the line Buchanan had drawn in the dirt. Beaumont tried to get attention, but it was to Buchanan that the people paid heed.

Buchanan said, "This is a bout under London Prize Ring Rules." He recited them from memory, pausing for emphasis. Now he had the mob listening. There were veteran observers among them who did not really know the fine points, the fact that wrestling was allowable to throw a man down, the fact that a fighter may not fall without being hit and other niceties.

He ended, "You see the line. Stay behind it, please. Patrol will be maintained by Billy Button . . ." There were jeers rather than cheers. ". . . and Miz Bea Johnson."

That took them by surprise. They

began to yell and wave their hats and flourish the bottles they had brought to maintain their spirits. Buchanan seized the opportunity to tell Beaumont to take over and to motion to Ed Avery for a conference.

Buchanan said, "I ain't sure which way the storm comes from, but I know clouds when I see 'em. If you and some of the miners could sorta keep a path aimed at town . . . I'll be movin' fast when this is over."

Avery said, "There'll be a riot if Coco wins."

Buchanan said, "Just be ready for anything."

Beaumont was posing, bringing the two fighters to scratch. The hot sun shone down. They appeared mismatched, the tall, well-built McMillan and the shorter, stocky Coco Bean. It was apparent that McMillan had all the confidence he needed, he grinned and waved to friends and backers. He shuffled, doing a bit of buck and wing as they were introduced.

Coco never glanced at his opponent.

His brown eyes were on Buchanan in his corner. He was watching Buchanan's hands making quick little motions. Beaumont called, "Time, gentlemen," and he went out to the mark at ring center. Beaumont poised a hand between them, then stepped back as a cowbell clanged, wielded by a neutral bystander.

Buchanan said, "Make that move! Now!"

McMillan danced out, long arm extended, aimed down at Coco's head. He was on his toes, boxing, his right hand cocked. He looked to be indomitable.

Coco made a little run, short steps, mincing. He ducked under the long left, slapped one to the body, moved outside. McMillan came again with the left jab from outside.

Coco made the move he had rehearsed with Buchanan. It was footwork—going against the dancing-boxing master with his own medicine. Coco retreated a step as if afraid of the long left.

Then he was inside with a speed that made men gasp. He slammed the left to the body. He drove his big, bare fist across from the right. He connected with the jaw.

Immediately he again lowered his sights. He sent a left hook and a right cross to the body.

McMillan was already falling. Coco hit him again on the chin for good measure. McMillan turned over from its force and rolled as he hit, winding up flat on his belly, his arms outspread. Beaumont, frozen, white-faced, stammered, forgetting to count.

Buchanan roared, "The winner! Give us the winner!"

Beaumont peered at McMillan. The big man lay as one dead. Buchanan grabbed Coco's right arm and raised it.

Beaumont pointed weakly at Coco and murmured something. The crowd was already turning into a mob. Fists flew as bettors rejected such an ending—or rejoiced in it. Buchanan was already running. Billy was with him.

Bea Johnson called, "Where to, big boy?"

"The bank!" Buchanan yelled. "Bring that old Mizer."

He and Billy leaped into the saddles. Coco, dragging the blanket, brow furrowed, fought his way to the buggy and climbed in. Nora was wide-eyed, watching her husband and Buchanan as they flew toward Encinal.

Buchanan sat firm in the saddle as Nightshade turned loose his enormous supply of speed. The bay could not keep up with such a pace and Billy fell behind. The buggy came behind with Nora now plying the whip. People strewed in a line, ragged, uncomprehending. The main body of the crowd stayed to drink and argue and battle.

The explosion blasted the clear air and sullied the town with billowing black clouds long before Buchanan hit the foot of Main Street. They had timed it well, he thought. If the fight had gone for an hour or so, as they had planned, they would be able to dispose of the loot at their leisure. Now he spoke to Nightshade, and the big black flew over the hard turf.

The fire bell clanged, but of course the volunteers were mainly at the prizefight. The smoke clouds began to evaporate and suddenly shots rang out. Ordinary citizens ran for cover.

Buchanan hit Main Street. Now he could see men kneeling and firing. He also heard a high, keening screech, which did not come from the lips of a white man.

So the Apaches had known; he had been right. He drew his revolver, gripped the reins in his teeth, and pulled the rifle from its scabbard. He rode down Main Street like an avenging angel. A shot tore his hat away.

He saw two men grappling in the dust of the street. One had an ordinary grain sack filled with something worth fighting over, since the second, a brown-skinned youth, was determined to yank it away. Bullets kicked up dust around them.

Buchanan rode them down, fired two shots at the battling little knot of men at the bank. Nightshade had kicked the embattled pair apart. Buchanan sheathed the rifle and made a running dismount, sending Nightshade out of danger with a slap on the flank.

He saw Billy coming in on the bay, the buggy not far behind. Away back came Bea Johnson in a carriage with Hamilton Mizer . . . and Marshal Beaumont.

He lost track of them then, going straight for the grain sack, which lay in the gutter. He picked it up and ran for the bank. It was still burning. He wheeled around. An Apache came at him. He shot low, bringing down the brave—one of the youths under Jo-san, he recognized. Then he saw Jo-san himself, who was aiming a .45 Colt at his head. He ducked, thinking at the same instant how ridiculous that was considering the speed of a bullet.

The revolver never went off. Billy Button flashed in on the bay. He dove from the saddle and hit Jo-san amidships. The gun flew away. Billy rolled in the dirt with the breed. They were of a size and weighed about the same, Buchanan thought, turning his attention elsewhere.

He saw Freddy Daggett and Dolan, then. They were making for the sack under his arm, each with a gun. They came at him and behind them limped Griff. Buchanan held his revolver steady on them.

"You want it, come and get it," he told them calmly. He had a good spot, he could see up and down the street. He saw the buggy come in, saw Coco dismount. Teresa and Nora and the baby drove on. He followed them with his gaze. He saw Juju and Emalita and the older Apaches leap from hiding.

He threw the sack of money at Daggett and the others. It had no value in the face of what was occurring. He ran down the street. Emalita was already climbing into the buggy.

Juju whirled around. He lifted a rifle. Buchanan did not hesitate. He shot Juju in the middle, regretting it but with no other choice.

He ran on. There were six more of

them, at the head of the horse, scrambling to get to the baby and Nora. Buchanan kept firing. One of them hit the dirt. Two more screamed, falling. Emalita made a grab for the baby, and Nora hit her with the butt of the buggy whip.

Emalita fell out of the buggy. The Apaches were huddled, dropping their arms, raising their hands. Down the street Coco was demolishing the young Apaches. Daggett and Griff and Dolan had vanished.

Billy and Jo-san were having it out. Billy seemed better at the fist fighting, but Jo-san used Indian wrestling tricks to throw him around the street. Hamilton Mizer staggered toward his bank, crying out for the law. Beaumont stayed with him, giving confused orders to which no one paid attention.

Buchanan went hot foot into the hotel. It was the logical place to find what he sought, he figured. Bea Johnson appeared. The saloon was deserted. She pointed to a door behind a potted fake rubber tree.

"Heloise boozes it up in there, big boy," she said, unrufled. "Better look out, though."

Buchanan said, "You be ready to duck." He set sail for the door, head lowered, shoulder hunched.

"Right with you, lover," Bea Johnson said. She picked up a long-necked liquor bottle.

Buchanan went through the door as though it were paper. A shot sounded, cut a lock of his hair. The three men were in the room. He fired twice, saw Griff and Daggett go down. He looked for Dolan, the gunman.

Dolan, canny, experienced, fired from behind the door. The bullet ripped Buchanan's shirt at heart level and seared across his ribs. Buchanan shot Dolan through the left eye.

Bea Johnson came into the room. Heloise was against the wall, white-faced, clutching the bag of loot from the bank. She lifted a small revolver.

Bea Johnson threw the bottle. It struck

Heloise alongside her head. She went down like a poled ox.

Buchanan said, "Thanks. I owe you one."

"She'd probably of missed," said Bea Johnson, never losing her cool demeanor. "Is that the stolen stuff?"

He said, "In the sack. Take care of it, will you?" He was already running for the street.

Bea Johnson said to herself, "You gotta be crazy, woman. Help yourself to some of this green stuff. Or at least a gold piece or two."

But she carried the sack out into the saloon, made certain it was tightly closed, and wandered out on the veranda to watch the proceedings.

Billy and Jo-san were still battling. It was the only remaining violence taking place. Beaumont was in front of the bank with Hamilton Mizer. The fire fighters were not able to stop the flames from consuming the bank. A wall fell in and Mizer held his hands over his face.

Buchanan went into the street. Coco

was circling the two young battlers, muttering encouragement to Billy.

"In the belly, kid. Now the head. Stick it in his eye. Don't let him grab you again!"

But Jo-san threw Billy over his head and pounded upon him. Billy, breathing hard, lifted a knee. Jo-san flew backwards. Emalita came staggering through the cloud of dust and backstopped her son. She was going past him and after Billy when Nora came racing with the buggy whip. Once more Emalita went down.

Billy saw what happened. A beatific smile adorned his features. While he exulted, Jo-san reached far back and swung a fist and hit him on the jaw. Billy went cartwheeling into Coco's grasp.

Out of the corner of his eye Buchanan caught a glimpse of McMillan. Wearing a jersey over his fighting tights, he was sneaking onto the porch of the hotel where Bea Johnson held the sack of loot. Beaumont was following him. The attention of the town was fully upon the other activities: the fire, Emalita and Nora, the fight between Billy and Josan.

Buchanan gave them time enough. Then he came from the opposite direction. McMillan was just laying hands upon Bea Johnson as Beaumont grabbed for the loot.

Buchanan asked, "Now, where the hell would you be going with that, anyway?"

McMillan came around with his fists up. Beaumont went for his revolver.

Buchanan kicked and the gun left Beaumont's grasp. Bea Johnson, showing neat footwork for a lady her size, caught it before it could hit the floor. She said, "Now, there, little man. At this distance I can't miss."

Beaumont bit his mustache, retreated with arms half-raised. Bea Johnson maneuvered so that she could watch Buchanan, never losing her wide smile.

McMillan led with the long jab, then tried a right low and below the belt. Buchanan moved slightly, easily. The jab missed. The right was blocked by Buchanan's knee.

McMillan crowded forward, the bigger man, intent on destroying his opponent with a barrage of blows from hamlike fists. He struck air as Buchanan danced out of reach. His upper body inclined, off balance.

Buchanan still smarted from the flight of the bullet that had burned him. It lent a definite impulse to his swinging right to the fleshy base of McMillan's jaw.

The prizefighter did a half turn, then stumbled. He pitched forward. For the second time that day he fell on his face. A chair splintered and he lay in the wreckage. Buchanan said to Beaumont, "You been lucky so far. Want to keep it that way?"

"I have committed no crime, suh." Beaumont was bleating, all his suavity had evaporated. "I do not know what is going on here, but I have no part in it. None, suh. None!"

"How about that?" demanded Bea Johnson. "Does he think Heloise, the darlin', and this big bloke, McMillan—and whoever else is left alive—won't be singing pretty little songs? Ho, ho, ho, as Santa says!"

Buchanan was again watching the fight in the dust of Main Street. Billy was on his knees. Jo-san was on his. They faced each other, swinging slowly, wearily, neither with enough strength left to knock over the other. Coco circled, keeping everyone away, encouraging Billy. Emalita, tough, again conscious and active, yelled for Jo-san to kill.

They were a lot alike, Buchanan thought. They were the rebellious young. No matter who won, however, Jo-san had the worst of it. His father was dead, he would be arrested and put in jail—death to Apaches, even half-Mexican Apaches.

Buchanan went down the steps. He leaned past Coco, saw that the boys were thoroughly exhausted. He reached out with huge hands and plucked them apart. He set them upon their feet, holding them erect on their rubber legs.

He said, "Enough." In Spanish he called over Emalita.

She came beside him, expressionless,

emotionless on the surface. "*Sí*, Buchanan."

"Take him and go. It better be the reservation."

"They will not accept me now."

"Mexico, then," said Buchanan. He reached and found his last gold piece— until he collected his winnings. He gave it to her. "Buy food for strength. Take horses at Billy's graze. I will send word. Stay out of sight until we can clean up the town."

"They will kill us."

"I said to git. Now git!" He released Jo-san, and Emalita put her arm around the youth and led him out of the crowd.

Buchanan said. "Ain't anybody goin' to help put out the fire?"

They turned, easily directed, as with all mobs. Coco came and stood and watched Emalita and the young man slide off Main Street down an alley.

He said, "That kid fought good."

"Yes." Billy was heaving for breath. Buchanan turned him over to Coco. "You two better see that Nora is okay."

"But . . . what happened?" asked Billy. "Where is everybody? What happened to the bank and all?"

Buchanan said, "In time, pretty soon. Go take care of your wife and baby."

Billy shook his head, clearing out the last cobweb. He wobbled down toward the carriage. Nora came down and reached out her arms.

"You fought fine," she cried. "You showed them!"

He said humbly, "I . . . couldn't . . . put him . . . away."

"You did good," she insisted. "Come on, now. Let's go home and fix your poor eye."

He touched a swelling eye with shaking fingers. He got into the buggy. Nora picked up the reins. They set off for the house on the hill, Teresa holding the baby, Billy holding the hand not occupied with the reins.

Buchanan turned back to the town. Avery was waiting for him. Mizer, shivering, scared, was behind him.

Lawyer Chatterton appeared from some recess where he had been hiding.

Avery said, "The badge. Would you take it, Tom?"

"No," said Buchanan. "Every time I put on a badge it means more trouble. I'm a peaceable man."

Avery did not smile. "I know, but . . ."

Buchanan beckoned them to the porch of the Palace Hotel. They came, eager to do his bidding.

He said, "There's part of the loot. The stakes money, everything. There's probably another bag in the back room. I don't think Heloise will be trying to depart with it."

"She should be wakin' up." Bea Johnson handed over the revolver she had appropriated and went indoors. Beaumont looked as though he had been plastered to the flashing of the hotel. Even his mustache had lost its dash, the ends turned down in defeat.

Buchanan said, "Ed, I think you should take over until an election can be held. You'll want to reorganize the town."

"It sure is kicked all to hell," said Avery. He tore the badge from Beaumont's vest, ripping the moiré silk material. "Reckon we can hold this one and his sister and McMillan for inquiry."

"There may be a couple of the others left alive. Which I doubt," Buchanan said.

Bea Johnson returned. She held a bedraggled Heloise at arm's length. Heloise had a whiskey bottle by the neck. As they came onto the veranda she took a healthy swig.

Bea Johnson said, "She came to, all right. Didn't try to run, though. Just got stiff as quick as possible. She always did have a habit."

Avery asked, "You want to confess now, Miss Beaumont?"

"Miss Beaumont, hell," Heloise said, slurring the word. "Miss Dare. Miss Heloise Dare. And the hell with you, all of you. I didn't do anything at all. I never set foot out of the hotel today. So . . . believe their lies if you want. I deny all!"

She made a wide gesture. Bea Johnson let go of her and she tottered several steps and fell over the prone McMillan. She blinked at him, then owlishly surveyed the others.

"Shay . . . tell me . . . who won the damn fight?"

Avery said, "She'll sober up in jail. I've got a couple miners I can appoint as deputies. We'll clean up, Tom. We'll total up the money and pay everyone off before nightfall."

"You do that," said Buchanan. He looked at Bea Johnson. Her white outfit was ruined. Only her cheerful countenance had remained clear and serene through the day. "Hey, you know what? We're goin' to get your stuff and you're goin' to use that bathroom after all."

She said, "Big boy, I believe you. Somethin' tells me you are the boss man today!"

They walked toward Billy's tent, arm

in arm. The town was in an immense flurry of activity. They ignored it.

Buchanan said, "Know what? I just won the mortgage on the hotel."

"It's a white elephant. Ain't it?"

"I wonder." He squeezed her arm. "I'm thinkin' about somethin'."

"Big boy, I'm thinkin' the same things."

He grinned at her. "No. I'm thinkin' that you could run that joint fine."

"In this town?"

"I don't mean with gals. I mean legitimate. I won enough cash to pay off the loan."

"And you'll stay and help?"

He shook his head. "Lady, I never stop anywhere very long. I might stay awhile." He was conscious again of the slight pain in his ribs. His shirt was sticking to his torso. "Coco might hang around awhile."

"Coco ain't mad at you anymore, I notice."

"He never was. He was just loyal to Nora and the baby. What with the fight and old Mizer sellin' land for farmin'—

good land, too—and Billy's graze and all, I think Encinal is about to go on the map."

"Talk on."

"You could run the Palace on shares. Keep it clean."

"Could I buy into it? I won aplenty too, you know, big boy. Plenty!"

"It's a deal." He held out a hand. "Shake."

They clasped and then he winced. She looked down and saw the way his shirt was sticking, saw the stain beneath his loose vest. They had come to the tent.

She said, "Big boy, come on inside."

"That's the ladies' section."

"Well, hell, I'll try to pass for a lady," she said, grinning once more. "What I want is to undress you."

He said, "Uh-huh. I knew you'd get around to it sometime."

"And put a bandage on you," she finished. "Hell, man, you just told me this was a respectable town."

They went into the tent. It was a time to settle down for a little while, he thought, admiring the full curves of her as she tore up white cloth for a bandage and came at him still grinning. It was more than time for a long loaf among his friends.

He said as she carefully removed his shirt, "And then there's the christenin' of Thomas Mulligan. Named for me and his grampaw, y' know."

"Christenin'? In a church?"

"They don't hold 'em in saloons!"

She took a deep breath. "Big boy, seems to me you've gone all the way."

"All the way?"

"I wanted to live on the level . . . But I never thought any big galoot would make me willin' to enter a church!"

He smiled at her. She surely was a big one and pretty as a picture, too. Like a picture he had seen on the wall of an opulent saloon . . .

WOLF DOG RANGE
by Lee Floren

Montana was big country, but not big enough for a ruthless land-grabber like Will Ardery. He would stop at nothing, unless something stopped him first—like a bullet from Pete Manly's gun.

Larry and Stretch: DEVIL'S DINERO
by Marshall Grover

Plagued by remorse, a rich old reprobate hired the Texas Troubleshooters to deliver a fortune in greenbacks to each of his victims. Even before Larry and Stretch rode out of Cheyenne, a traitor was selling the secret and the hunt was on.

CAMPAIGNING
by Jim Miller

Ambushed on the Santa Fe trail, Sean Callahan is saved from dying by two Indian strangers. Then the trio is joined by a former slave called Hannibal. But there'll be more lead and arrows flying before the band join the legendary Kit Carson in his campaign against the Comanches.

DONOVAN
by Elmer Kelton

Donovan was supposed to be dead. The town had buried him years before when Uncle Joe Vickers had fired off both barrels of a shotgun into the vicious outlaw's face as he was escaping from jail. Now Uncle Joe had been shot—in just the same way.

CODE OF THE GUN
by Gordon D. Shirreffs

MacLean came riding home with saddle-tramp written all over him, but sewn in his shirt-lining was an Arizona Ranger's star. MacLean had his own personal score to settle—in blood and violence!

GAMBLER'S GUN LUCK
by Brett Austen

Gamblers hands are clean and quick with cards, guns and women. But their names are black, and they seldom live long. Parker was a hell of a gambler. It was his life—or his death . . .

ORPHAN'S PREFERRED
by Jim Miller

A boy in a hurry to be a man, Sean Callahan answers the call of the Pony Express. With a little help from his Uncle Jim and the Navy Colt .36, Sean fights Indians and outlaws to get the mail through.

DAY OF THE BUZZARD
by T. V. Olsen

All Val Penmark cared about was getting the men who killed his wife. All young Jason Drum cared about was getting back his family's life savings. He could not understand the ruthless kind of hate Penmark nursed in his guts.

THE MANHUNTER
by Gordon D. Shirreffs

Lee Kershaw knew that every Rurale in the territory was on the lookout for him. But the offer of $5,000 in gold to find five small pieces of leather was too good to turn down.

RIFLES ON THE RANGE
by Lee Floren
Doc Mike and the farmer stood there alone between Smith and Watson. Doc Mike knew what was coming. There was this moment of stillness, a clock-tick of eternity, and then the roar would start. And somebody would die . . .

HARTIGAN
by Marshall Grover
Hartigan had come to Cornerstone to die. He chose the time and the place, but he did not fight alone. Side by side with Nevada Jim, the territory's unofficial protector, they challenged the killers—and Main Street became a battlefield.

HARSH RECKONING
by Phil Ketchum
The minute Brand showed up at his ranch after being illegally jailed, people started shooting at him. But five years of keeping himself alive in a brutal prison had made him tough and careless about who he gunned down . . .

FIGHTING RAMROD
by Charles N. Heckelmann

Most men would have cut their losses, but Frazer counted the bullets in his guns and said he'd soak the range in blood before he'd give up another inch of what was his.

LONE GUN
by Eric Allen

Smoke Blackbird had been away too long. The Lequires had seized the Blackbird farm, forcing the Indians and settlers off, and no one seemed willing to fight! He had to fight alone.

THE THIRD RIDER
by Barry Cord

Mel Rawlins wasn't going to let anything stand in his way. His father was murdered, his two brothers gone. Now Mel rode for vengeance.

RIDE A LONE TRAIL
by Gordon D. Shirreffs

The valley was about to explode into open range war. All it needed was the fuse and Ken Macklin was it.

ARIZONA DRIFTERS
by W. C. Tuttle
When drifting Dutton and Lonnie Steelman decide to become partners they find that they have a common enemy in the formidable Thurston brothers.

TOMBSTONE
by Matt Braun
Wells Fargo paid Luke Starbuck to outgun the silver-thieving stagecoach gang at Tombstone. Before long Luke can see the only thing bearing fruit in this eldorado will be the gallows tree.

HIGH BORDER RIDERS
by Lee Floren
Buckshot McKee and Tortilla Joe cut the trail of a border tough who was running Mexican beef into Texas. They stopped the smuggler in his tracks.

HARD MAN WITH A GUN
by Charles N. Heckelmann
After Bob Keegan lost the girl he loved and the ranch he had sweated blood to build, he had nothing left but his guts and his guns but he figured that was enough.

...MBLER

...nning away
...dead man's
place. No matter what he decided he was
bound to end up dead.

THE GUNSHARP
by William R. Cox

The E........ weren't very smart. They
tra.......................d
Ar...

W...
G...
so...
ar...
to...

S...
a...
h...
a...